THE CHOOSING

You gonna choose
up or get trampled?

Khalidah J. Hunter

authorHOUSE®

AuthorHouse™
1663 Liberty Drive
Bloomington, IN 47403
www.authorhouse.com
Phone: 1 (800) 839-8640

Published by AuthorHouse   04/08/2016

ISBN: 978-1-5246-0222-2 (sc)
ISBN: 978-1-5246-0221-5 (e)

CONTENTS

This book is dedicated to my Nana Carroll Ann Johnson.
Thank You for loving me even when I didn't love myself.
My brother Vaughn Rollins.
Even when no one else believed, you always knew the truth.
Rest Easy

CHAPTER 1
Her

I know your reading this title like, uh, not another one. Not another chick talking about getting cheated on. Awwww, boo hoo! Sooooo sad! Nah, it's not even like that. It's what you hear about and but us women never speak about. How a real bitch moves in silence, does her dirt and sweeps it under the rug. About how after years of fucking around and a series of relationships, flings, and fucking's couldn't change me. I am who, I am, a mom, sister, aunt, writer, lover, fighter. But most of all I'm a cheater. But before you sit there and judge me, everybody has made questionable decisions. We all have pulled our inner smut out and did smut like things. It's just I'm woman enough to admit it. I like my freaky inner bitch that takes what she wants. With that being said, let me lay the groundwork so you understand. I'm sure you can relate, even though you might not want to admit it. And fuck the bullshit; I take responsibility for never being monogamous, EVER.

It's easy for people to say, I'm a product of my environment, I was never loved enough, I ain't have no daddy around, blah, blah, blah. Please!!! What can I say, it's all true. But make no mistake, none of that shit played a role in which I became. I liked the rush of potentially being caught. I like the creep and set-up. I like to get those kinky pics and "I want to taste you" text. I hear dudes saying, Ain't nothing like pussy but some new pussy. Not the same for most cocks! New dudes run the risk of being real regular with the dick, way less than spectacular. I consider myself a top shelf cock connoisseur. Meaning I only fuck with high quality cock and you have impeccable eatta skills. No half stepping for this twat. Putting a bland dick in here is like smoking Reggie. Would never put that BS in my lungs, so why accept a limp dick? Anyway that's neither here, nor there; never would I say my life was easy, because it never was. But maybe you feel like you need something to justify my actions.

My biological mother had 3 kids with 3 baby daddies. She never raised us; she left that up to her mother, my Nana. She raised me and siblings up until she died of a stroke just shy of her 63rd birthday. Even though my grandparents raised us, we saw Tracey from time to time, between jail stints and rehab. I was never bitter about the situation; almost everyone who was born in the 80's was raised by someone other than their parents. I was just like any kid whose mom and dad abandoned them, I just wanted to be with my mom. At the time I didn't understand how a person could be so selfish and not feel her heart strings tug, I would cry at night for her. Until my Nana heard me one night, she smacked the shit out of me. "What the fuck you crying over a person who's too wrapped in themselves to love the gifts that God gave her?" Nana Ann would say. See what I didn't realize then, was my mother was a junkie. She had a really bad habit and the only thing that saved her life was periodical stays in jail. Now Nana loved her some Tracey, whether she was dressed in the finest or walking around with rags hanging off her ass. Tracey was my Nana's oldest child and only daughter out of 6 kids. Even though she told Tracey after the first 2 kids she took from the hospital she wasn't raising anymore, Tracey still had another baby. Tracey didn't care then and still doesn't care now. I take that back, she cares she just doesn't know how to show it. But it never matter because Nana Ann loved us unconditionally and showered us with attention. The only thing is she could be strict, mean, and cold when needed. And she made it her business to make sure that I didn't end up like Tracey. She had me convinced that she was all knowing, and seeing. I guess that's why when all my friends were fucking like rabbits; I was scared to death she would know immediately that some guy had busted my little ass. So I waited, planned, and picked who the guy would be. I made sure I took precautions, because I ain't see no kids in my future, because I never wanted to be like Tracey. We were more alike than even I can admit. But looking back, I can say her ways def rubbed off on me. Like I said she had 3 babies, I'm the 2nd child, and 1 of 2 daughters. And while everyone else was living it up, I worked weekends and after school to get the things I wanted. I always felt different about what was expected and how to conduct myself. And for years I did exactly what was needed to make everyone happy. But then things started to change, my body changed, and that's when I felt that first sense of longing.

My siblings and I always knew that we all had different dads just by looking at us. We ranged from the deepest milk chocolate to the lightest cream with every shade in between. We are beautiful and we all look alike. When we get together its nothing but laughs, jokes and good times all around. Don't get it twisted, we still beef. But at the end of the day this is like CMB, we all we got. We ride for one another and snap when it's necessary. And even though we don't always agree, it's always from a place of love and never hate. We don't need no team cause we are an army. Fuck wit us or fuck off! We were taught that if one beefs, we all beef or get your ass beat.

The bitches that I keep in my immediate circle are more like sister's to me. I've known these hoes (as a term of endearment) since we were still rocking training bras. I love them, and these bitches love me. Sometimes we go for months without talking, but when we link up it's like we were just together yesterday. So even though I'm not on the phone busting it up with them every day I know what it is with us. It's Peyton, my bitch since we were 12 years old stuffing our bras. TaTa, my little sister by 2 years that has always been my irk and heart at the same damn time. Shiana, we got close after we graduated high school and realized we had so much in common. With these three girls around, it's like 4 the hard way. We come, fuck shit up, and leave. I can't help if I love bad bitches, that my fucking problem! So we might not always hang, but when we do, we are the party! Dudes gravitate around us, and bitches want to be us. SO when we go out we give them something to stare at, fucking haters. Just know that if we show up, it's about to be way turned up! #turndownforwhat

And then there was me, Kennedy. As I'm writing this I am currently embarking on my 27th birthday. That bald headed bitch, 30, is kicking in the door and making her presence known. I wouldn't say that I'm concerned about my age, because I know I still look like a teeny bopper. I'm 5 feet 11 inches, 132lbs, light skinned like somebody stopped the toaster half way thru. Yeah, I'm a tall glass of water and no I'm not a model or I didn't play ball. I'm tall, thin, and fabulous. I love my body, flaws and all. And the men can't get enough of me! My face is so serene most people think I'm too pretty to pout but I curse like a sailor. My sense of humor is that of a woman who has an older brother and has always been surrounded by men, it's lewd, crude, and x rated. So once you put that all together, sprinkle some nail polish, lashes, and stilettos you got one bad bitch. Not just aesthetically. I'm hard working, independent, selfless, willing, and a motivator. She acts like a lady but def thinks like a man. And that's where you mother fuckers are going to have a problem, the mindset of a dude. #phuckyoopinion Shit it's my life! I'm, living it like it's golden.

So yeah, I got a gang a bitch and a few associates I fuck wit but my circle is so small I feel like I'm talking to myself most of the time. Plus these bitches want to be you and live your life. I don't have time for that shit and I will bust a chick head for trying to be slick. Just because I'm cute don't mean you won't get dropped! Not only is that a true story but I'm dead ass serious. Mind your business and we won't have a problem. Understood? Now back to what I was saying, got me all riled up talking about these THOTS. Oh, so yeah I'm that deal and so is my girls. Now even though these are my homies, I don't think they realize how far the treachery goes. I mean, I am a serial monogamous. I like (pause) love that shit! So even though they think they know me and all my dudes, they really have no idea of who I am underneath all the clothes and jewels. It's crazy to think that I change up like a switch that clicks on and off depending on who's in the room. And I keep certain things separate just like my laundry. Everybody can't be together because they don't mesh well without consequences. So just when I thought everything was going well, the raggedy ass bitch, Karma, decided to rear her ugly head. And man oh man, that Karma bitch is thee baddest bitch of them all. This is how the end became the beginning, how being slick can make your ass slide right down a slide with razor blades on it. Yeah get that picture in your mind, because the truth hurts and it sure ain't pretty either.

The place: The realist streets of Atlantic City, New Jersey. Where the weather is just like the people, temperamental. Where rappers never come up and kingpins always go to jail. Where rats all swear their loyalty while their names are coming up in Green sheets. A city where your new baby mom's is probably your man's old baby moms. A place where it's cool to be high and dumb to try to rise above it all. Yep, AC aka 609 was where I was born and raised. Jersey made me but wouldn't break me.

I met Carlos when I was 16 years old. I had been in SC for the summer with my aunts and cousins. I couldn't wait to get back home after being dumped by my summer boyfriend Mike. Shit was going good until someone new moved on the block. Not only did he meet her, he took her home to meet his family, knocked the dirty bitch up and married her all before they turned 18. I was devastated, crushed emotionally, and wanted fucking revenge. But when I look back on it, I'm also grateful, I dodged that bullet of being stuck down south pushing out babies whenever the wind blew to hard. I mean who drops me when I look way better than her? Well in my mind, at that young immature age, I thought looks were all that mattered besides not having kids. I thought I was a great catch and he was an idiot. It turned out he was, but by then it wasn't my problem any longer. So I was in a funk. I wanted to meet someone but had never been into talking to random dudes and dating. For one, my Nana didn't play that shit, and for two,

I was still young and had my whole life ahead of me. I mean hey, I had dudes chasing me, but I wasn't interested in any of them.

That was until I met him, the dude that would change my life, Carlos. At first I didn't notice him, but obviously he noticed me and fancied me. The day I came back from SC in a bad ass mood, I figured I would go check my best friend. I missed her something crazy and couldn't wait to catch up on the local gossip that I missed. As I approached her yard, there was this fine ass dude sitting there like he was waiting for someone. I had never seen him before and knew that if I did, I would remember him. When I asked him who he was looking for, he said my best friend. That he had just moved into the old Miller house on the corner with his mom and sisters. It was something about his eyes that had me mesmerized when he talked to me. See he was a hustler, a real dope boy. His mom was a single mother and his father had never been around. When the chips are down and you're hungry, you'll do anything to survive. So he sold that shit from sun up to sun down, never slept always on the grind. Change, cash, food stamp card, if you got anything for collateral, he got that work. He never ran with a crew because he never wanted the problems, so he ran DOLO. His goal was to be that "Guy", said he didn't care if he went to jail as long as he was eating like a king on the streets. He knew that when the cops finally did catch him, he would be going to Club FED, with football numbers behind his name. When we met, he was just on the come up, street dealer level, but with his ambition and drive, I knew that he would be paid eventually. I liked that, I liked him and how people respected me knowing that he was my dude. Even though I was only a teenager, I knew what that life entailed, so I always kept my grades and worked an after school job. Money was never an issue and the sky was the limit. See I didn't fall for him on sight, no. I wasn't interested in his money because I was always taught to make my own. We played this game of acting like we couldn't feel the electricity between the two of us until I couldn't resist anymore. He and Peyton already had their own thing going on, and I wasn't into stepping on toes. Even though I knew he liked me, she was my best friend. So after a night of truth of dare, I told Peyton I wanted him. She said they were just friends and I should go for it. I let him think that he was chasing me, when I was really fiending for him. When he asked me out again, I said yes. After that, we became inseparable; where ever I wasn't busy, I was with him. When he wasn't bussing moves, he was with me.

For my 17 birthday he brought me a car. He had moved to the next town over because he was racking in the cash. The car was so I could come and see him without waiting for anyone to bring me. He gave me key to his place so I could come and go as I please. He wanted me and he wanted me to himself. These were the early days, when we were still madly in love with each other. Before we both got too comfortable. Nights well spent watching him while he came and went as he made moves or while I studied. I remember rolling a fat one lying in the bed waiting for him to come in and just bust my ass. He was my outlet and a huge change from the mundane. That fast life and fast money had my heart racing. You ever get fucked in the trap with your back against the wall, with thousands on the table and the work ready to be bagged? That's the type of shit we was on. I couldn't get enough, and the more I gave the more he took. It was a mixture of fear and excitement to be around him. Fear that it could all go horribly wrong, excitement that he was getting away with doing something wrong. The thoughts about what if just made my pussy wet. He said he didn't really want this life but this life had chosen him. We talked about life after hustling and how transition into a more legal life. We both wanted more than we had growing up and both had the drive and ambition to make it happen. It was no surprise when I ended up pregnant; it was just seemed like it was happening so fast. A little over two years of us ripping and running, I ended up pregnant. The anxiety in telling him was so great I thought I was going to be sick to my stomach. I mean we lived a crazy lifestyle, early mornings with later nights. My emotions were mixed on the subject; I was all over the place. One minute scared, next nervous. But overall, even though I was 20 yrs old, I was still excited. I was ready to be a mom and something like a wife. I had already raised everyone else's kids, now I would have my own child. And I just kept thinking how one failed relationship opened up the door for a new beginning.

Now I know yall are shaking yall's head like "Why would she fuck with a drug dealer?" See Carlos aka Los, had it just as rough or if not rougher than me growing up. Growing up on the streets of Boston had turned him into a monster. This was not the life he chose but a couple wrong decisions lead him to this place. His mother raised him and his siblings alone on welfare. Where there was never enough, never enough food, never enough money, never enough time. He knew that his options were either dead or in jail. He said he would grind until he was rich, put him in a casket or they hauled him into Club FED. Los said he was bout that life didn't have a reason to get his life together because real niggas do real things. Hearing that conviction in his voice gave me glimpse into just how hard he had it. That was until we found out about Samya. His whole thought process changed, the way he looked at the world changed from black to grey. Everything wasn't a clean cut as he first wanted to believe life could be. Sleepless nights on how to maneuver so that he could still provide for us plagued his mind every time he closed his eyes. Until he woke up one morning and said enough was enough. I was almost six months pregnant, and was ready to get somewhere untainted by his business and get ready for my baby to come. The money that he used to re-up, he invested in local cleaners. That way he could wash his dirty money and have a legit income. He decided that this would be his exit out of the game. That he didn't want to be the father that he never had. That he would do right by us so that we as a family could have a great life. He owed it to himself to be a better person in general. This precious baby growing in my stomach that was half him and half me, she would be best of both of us. We owed it this child to give it the best we had to offer.

So we moved in and set up shop. Moving from Atlantic City to Absecon was like a culture shock even though it's only 15 minutes away the mentality is a whole world away from each other. It was so different from living in my hood that it took me months just to stay home without company. It wasn't anymore walking up the block to hang with my girls or going to get food at 4 am from the pizza spot on Pacific. But I needed the change, Los needed that change. I mean you can't start a family spending 90% of your time in the drug spot around fiends. I dropped out of college because my heart wasn't in it. My grandma passed away, she was my encourager, and I did that for her. So that she could have a chance to see one of her grandkids make it out of AC. Even though I know she would have wanted me to finish mentally I couldn't focus on how to get to the finish line. So I worked afternoons and he ran the cleaners in the daytime. For a while everything was good, the two of us. We had a life and we had a child on the way, cars, jewels, everything. My life was looking good, I felt like everything was finally coming together for me. But we all know that, that's not quite how life works. Then that bitch Karma came back.

Los had a case from before we ever met and had been going back and forth to court for three years. So he confesses his sins to me one night while I'm seven months pregnant and tells me he might have to go away eventually. That sometimes the past won't rest until it gets retribution and the law was one of those bitches that always had to cum first and cum the hardest. The DA was talking ridiculous numbers for a petty ass possession charge. But Los was smart, because he was like a chess player. Thinking of the opponent's next move before he even anticipated what they should do. Buying the business, going to NA meetings telling them he had a substance abuse problem, and hiring a lawyer that cost a grip and got all charges almost thrown out. He ended up beating the case but having to complete an outpatient drug program instead. His stipulations required him to do NA meetings and submit weekly drug testing for the duration of the program. He had the streets in him and just couldn't stay completely off the block, that's how he fed himself for years. Old habits are so hard to change but he was aiming. When the cleaners wasn't doing the numbers that he thought they should he was right back to making moves. He figured that that program was taking money out of his pockets and food off his table. And even though he went legit getting that slow money he still had his hand in the game

9

stirring the pot. He ended up getting arrested during a traffic stop for not having all his proper paperwork on him. This allowed the cops to check his vehicle finding a 8ᵗʰ of Bud for his self to smoke. To find out that he had a warrant for never even starting the program that he agreed too. This all happened when I was 8 months pregnant, emotional and worried. I was distraught and angry that I would be in a situation like this, but I was a survivor and I had so much more to live for now. Getting on my Geek shit I wrote a letter to the prosecutor and judge. I pulled out all of my SAT words to make him sound like he was reformed and had quit that life style. That he was a business owner, a soon to be father and was trying to become an upstanding citizen in the community. The aim was to get all the charges dropped and the least I was trying to do was get him a suspended sentence so he could be there for the birth of our first child. The letter accomplished what I wanted; he ended up with a suspended sentence that allowed him to be there for his family even if only for a short while. I may have not completed my degree, but I still had the gift of gab. And the mouth that always got me in trouble growing up saved him. Now it was just a waiting game: so while he was happy and I was anxious.

On June 22, only 2 weeks after Los got his suspended sentence, at 5:12 am we welcomed our baby girl into this world. 7 lb 6 oz of curly black hair and eyes just like her father. Samina CarrollAnn Cruz was the most beautiful baby I had ever laid eyes on and she was all mines. It was surreal to think that we made this kid and would be responsible for her. In an instant we went from being 2 to being 3. Looking in Carlos' eyes I seen a look of joyful fulfillment that I never seen until he seen her. And from that moment forward, it was about him and his princess Samya.

10 months.

That was all that me and Samya had with him when it was time for him to go to away. Even though I knew what to expect the shock of it was enough to make me angry. It didn't matter that it was planned and that this was what needed to be done so that he never had to leave us again. I never imagined that I would be a single mom with a dude that was away serving a bid. Even if it was a six month stint I still felt betrayed. I didn't want to break up our little family. For the last 6 months it had been only us, no family, and no friends, just us in our own little world. But that's the price you pay for wanting to come up. Nothing is for free, everything cost whether it be in monetary value or time. And now they wanted him to pay up by serving his sentence. His squad wanted to send him off with a bang, let him know that they had him. Food, drinks, bitches, mad neighborhood flunky's and weed were plentiful for his send off. We shut the whole block down, hired a fiend to man the grill and a DJ to keep everyone dancing well into the morning. Then we went home and hand a special party, just me and him. We made love like we wouldn't get a chance to touch each other ever again. All the while the clock was ticking away towards that inevitable deadline. And after we had our fill of each other we just lay in each other's arms and talked. He knew that it was a lot of fake love and real hate in these streets. He knew that once the food and liquor was gone, so would they. It's funny because everyone shows up for the party but nobody shows up to do the bid. I knew that all of these fair weather friends and family would disappear once he got locked down. But I let him have his regal moment because it gets really quiet on the inside.

Being a single mom was the hardest thing that I ever had to become. It was a thankless 24 hour job that instills fear and exhaustion into parents everywhere. Between working, the baby, visits, and phone calls I was frustrated. I missed my dude, I missed having someone around to talk to and joke with, someone to share my darkest fears and greatest hopes with, just someone who was there for me. I missed Carlos, but mostly I missed the sex. When Samya was in bed, and I was all alone with nothing but the TV to keep me company, was my favorite time of night. My imagination would get the best of me, it had me reminiscing about how he could make me cum every time we fucked had me in a constant state of arousal. I resulted into buying multiple toys to keep me satisfied without the temptation to sleep with someone else. Just thinking of him had me looking thru my box of toys until I found the one that would work for the fantasy. I lit some candles, and turned on some music. I was already horny, but I wanted to pretend he was here with me. Just when I got to the good part Carlos' phone started ringing.

Now he had already been away for a little over three weeks and had left all of his possessions with me. I left the phone on by accident and figured that everyone already knew that he was doing his bid. On a humbug I answered his phone because the number was saved under Tony. But as soon as I answered I knew that it wasn't a dude because I could hear the chicks laughing in the background. So instead of me getting defensive, I asked her who she was and what she wanted. She had the nerve to say she had the wrong number. Wrong number my ass, saved under a dudes name?! My emotion started getting the best of me and I wanted answers. Of course I called her back and asked her how she knew my dude. Of course she was a rowdy no class having School House bitch that was just being loud and obnoxious. Now that shit really pissed me off! My attitude instantly went from feeling sad about him being away to wanting to kill him. All types of thoughts start running thru my head questioning what he was doing in these streets. Like was he really out handling business or laid up with the next bitch? I'm here with your child, by myself and you have these dirty girls calling you? What exactly was their point? Like really cause if they fucking around then she needs to do this bid with him. Of course she pleads the 5th and said they we're just friends that like to smoke together. To me that was worse than her saying he fucked me dumped me. That means you were sitting around this bitch and her friends being friendly, taking money out of our house to hang with a bunch of hoes. That phone call was the catalyst, that phone call broke me. I was a new mom, still trying to get into the swing of things, and the person that was supposed to be by my side betrayed me. He traded my unconditional love for some broke ass hoe that wouldn't even write you back in jail.

The thing that ate me up the most about the situation was because he was in prison and I couldn't even confront him! This wasn't a phone call or letter type conversation, this required me looking into his and watching his body language when he spoke. That meant my emotions and anger had a chance to stew while I waited for our weekly visit. My mind raced with all types of scenarios, and little things he did. It seemed like I could find flaws in everything that he ever said or did. All the little white lies he told to keep me safe seem like big lies to cover up the fact you were trying to see someone else.

That week I experienced physical hell on earth. I had literally been sick since I spoke with her and felt like I couldn't rest until I got to the bottom of the situation. My stomach was constantly roiling, pounding headaches and physical pain in my chest where my heart used to be. The really sad thing is I knew even if what they both said was true, I wouldn't believe them. I mean I felt like a completely broken woman who let the guise of pillow talk promises lead me to believe that he was true. I was hoping for the best but I was prepared for the worst. Time seemed to be at a standstill, and as the hours turned into days, I knew that the outcome wasn't going to be in my favor.

• • • • • • • • ● • • • • • • • • •

It was the reaping. With nothing but time and opportunity, I was prepared mentally for war with him. I was going to make him remember why he was with me and what he would be losing at the same time. What he didn't realize is that he was in jail, I was free. I could come and go as I please, while is ever move was monitored and planned out for him. Looking my best, hair done, nails done, lip gloss on sauce, I looked way better than I felt. He needed to believe that this girl couldn't and can't fill my spot. I wouldn't give him the satisfaction to see me looking like how I felt on the inside, broken. After dressing myself and dropping Samya off to Peyton, I got on the road to make the 2 hour drive to see him. Blasting Keisha Cole at max level, because niggas, I should have cheated for all this drama. Sitting in the waiting room listening to the hoods scream at their kids, my anxiety started flare up in anticipation of the confrontation. I was a nervous wreck cause in my mind this was the dissolution of our relationship. One side of my rational brain was telling me to calm down and get the facts first, the irrational side was telling me to pop off before he could even fix his lips to lie to me. But my truth and his truth we're two different things.

The whole before I could see him was nothing but reflection for me. When I think back to his behavior I should of known that something was up. Little things that hold no meaning at the time but now seem so significant like the petty arguments for no reasons, accusations about where I've been and who I was with or any excuse to just to get out the house because he felt like I was nagging him. Long ago I chalked it up to us being young and inexperienced, both trying to find our way together. This was my 1st long term relationship with someone let alone had a baby with someone. I wanted it to work and I wanted my family to stay together. The love that I had for Los had never waned; it was just being smothered by the hate in my heart over this situation. The only way for me to get rid of the hurt was to inflict the same kind of pain on him. It didn't make it right, but I knew that it would make us even.

Sitting with my legs crossed, with the toe of my Nikes tapping out a rhythm on the floor. My nerves were on high alert as I waited in the visiting room to look Los in his eyes. Taking one last glimpse around the waiting room, I can feel his presence before I even look up. When he sees me his face lights up into a smile that outshines the dingy light bulbs hanging from the ceiling. He look on my face told him something was wrong before I spoke any words.

"Hey babe", said Los.

I just sat there with a blank stare on my face, with the girl's number written on a piece of paper. Proof, I had that. Waiting gave me the upper hand, he had no idea that I even knew about this girl.

"Babe?" he repeated.

"Who the fuck is Stacy?" Kennedy said.

"Stacy?! I don't know nobody named Stacy!" Los said. I just put my hand up to stop the litany of excuses he was going to try to come up with.

"Look, she's been calling your phone. Texting you, leaving you messages about coming thru to blow. I'm not beat, after all that I've been through with you, you got the nerve to entertaining some nothing hoes?!" Kennedy screamed at him, shoving the paper with her name and number in his face. The look on his face said it was more than a smoke buddy or someone he was just chilling with.

"Kennedy? She's nobody. She's just someone that I grew up with. I swear! I would never do you like that "Los said.

"Whelp, I hope she can do this bid with you because I am done! Tell her to drive two hours every week, accept your phone calls and keep your commissary stocked!" Kennedy stated as she stomped away.

"Babe! Babe! Please just listen to me! Give me a chance to explain!" Standing next to the door waiting for visiting hours to be over I just stared out the door with tears streaming down my face. I knew that it could come to this, but I couldn't believe the look of recognition that raced across his face when he seen the number. I just wanted to get home, have a drink, smoke an L, and hold my daughter. My resolve over the year's issues was starting to crumble. This visit put me in a bad place, with wicked thoughts. Being in bad places makes you make bad decision under the guise that this was life. In the grand scheme of things, I knew this a minor blip in the game of life. But at that moment it felt like my life damn near ended.

Your mind can be your worst enemy when you're in a bad place. My heart was pounding with sweaty palms from the anger pouring out of me. But it was more than that, it was shame that I was stupid, and betrayal because it never crossed my mind to cheat on him. Self evaluation made me realize that this guy was crazy, he had to be! I mean come on, I'm flying! Not just materialistically, mentally too. I was street and book smart, could jest with the best of them, could drink men under the table. I was the whole package, beauty and brains. It was dudes waiting and wanting an opportunity to even talk to me. Love had me blinded and it never crossed my mind to stray. Sliding my shades over my eyes to hide the tears, swiped on a fresh coat of MAC lip glass, sashaying like my hips birthed the world; I hopped in my car speeding down the Expressway and could only think of one word over and over again: PAYBACK!

CHAPTER 2
The Big Payback

Racing back home with the windows down and music up I was angry. Angry at him, angry at myself, and angry that I didn't see what was going on right under my nose. Like seriously Kennedy, how could you be so oblivious to the way he moved? Or wonder why he always wanted to start an argument about dumb shit when there wasn't a reason? Now I understand looking back in retrospect. He always wanted to piss me off so that he could have a reason to leave and run the streets. He always wanted me to himself. Trying to alienate me so I wouldn't have a shoulder to cry on but I was never stupid. My friends loved me fiercely and understood that my life was taking a different path but always made their presence known. Never allowing him to scare them or intimidate them enough that they would just fade into the background. Today I was grateful because I needed them more now than ever before.

Back home after hours of crying and a migraine on high alert I had an opportunity to think and ponder. I thought about the direction my life was heading in and the decisions that I made. I thought about Los and how his actions affected our family. I thought about being oblivious to what is right in front of my eyes. I thought about how stupid I was to just sit back and let the chips fall where they may. Days literally flew past where I was just in auto pilot. Get Baby to the daycare, work, store, pick baby up, home repeat. Los would still write like normal, he would still try to call. I would look at the caller ID and just put the phone back down. Bottles on bottles of wine helped to numb the pain. And hopefully make me not dream about him. Then those nights I was just up staring at the walls, trying to figure out a way to make the pain stop. Day to day, I was going thru the motions just barely holding it together. Walking around like everything is fine when deep down all you want to do is just lay somewhere and sleep away your problems. The days were easy to manage with all the busy work, but the nights were damn near unbearable. Tossing and turning all night while the images that you conjure dance behind your eyelids. Trying to shut off your brain while a million thoughts are running through your head is like trying to stop a runaway train going full speeds ahead. Heart racing at the thought that mother fuckers really weren't who they claim to be. Mother fuckers had hidden agendas and motives for why they keep you around. I don't know if what I thought or was thinking was true or real. I just knew how I felt and I just didn't want to feel that way anymore. I was tired of giving energy to a dead situation.

The decision was made to not go see him anymore until he came home. Los didn't deserve to see my face or hear my voice if he was going to keep this charade up. My anger was still at an all time high and I wasn't in the mood to fake like everything was okay or that it would be ok. I knew that this was the best for me, for my sanity. Then I realized that it would be selfish of me to take his daughter away from him. Los knew I would never put a strain on his relationship with his child, I knew how much that meant to him. The easiest solution was asking Peyton if she would take Mina and she agreed. She and Los had always had a good relationship; sometimes they seemed closer than me and her. So he started calling Peyton to talk to his daughter, and twice a week she would take her to visit. It worked out for me, and he still got a chance to see his baby girl. My heart still hurt and I didn't know how to face him without be angry.

Then I had an awakening.

I woke up one day and it was like a light bulb went off where the darkness was taking up space in my head. My mind didn't jump straight to thoughts about him and this situation. I started to feel better and lighter, I started to see clearer than I had in a long time. The thoughts and visions that consumed me of revenge became a whisper through my mind. I just wanted, no needed the companionship. I wanted a lover, somebody to make me forget about all the bullshit. I wanted somebody to fuck me and make me remember how it feels to be consumed in passion. Someone to kiss me and hold me and tell me everything was going to be alright. To take away all rational thoughts so that all exist is pure lust. I wanted someone that could make me remember and forget all at the same time. I wanted rough and kinky sex with no strings attached. I guess you could tell by my stance and attitude that I was open to take on a partner.

I had been thin my whole life except for when I was pregnant. But the bounce back was real; my body had never looked so filled out. I had thickness in all right place, but that was about all I had working for me at the moment. My hair was limp, nails unpainted, and skin dull. I looked like how I felt on the inside, like someone ran me over. I damn sure wasn't walking around flaunting myself like a proud peacock. Feathers plumed revealing all my colors, making it hard to not stop and stare at the light radiating from within. I was just the opposite, unremarkable and very forgettable. It was time to put my life back in order and get my appearance up to par. With Carlos in jail I didn't really have a reason to get cute at first. But now since I had no intention on seeing him until he came home, it was time for me to get right. My appearance affected my psyche which was a direct view on how other seen me. I hated myself and what I become, a self loathing ass female crying over a baby dad that could give 2 fucks bout how I felt. If he did care it was absolutely nothing he could do about it in jail. Catching a glimpse of my reflection on the computer monitor I decided to make some appointments: Hair, nails and Eyebrows. Walking into my boss's office I asked her if I could leave early to get a jump on getting my life back in order. She happily agreed shooing me out her office. All the while saying, I wondered when my real assistant was coming back, because dressed down Kennedy wasn't her assistant.

• • • • • • • ● • • • • • • • •

After spending the day and half the night getting curled, cut, and poked I felt like treating baby girl and myself to some water ice. Dead smack middle of the summer, sweat dripping between my breast, eyes covered in the darkest shades, white tank top with linen shorts, MK sandals on my feet, with a dab of Mac lip gloss to complete my whole look. Samya was rocking her clear jellies and pink sundress. She had just had her first birthday blowout where Aunties and God Mommy went crazy with the gifts. She had so many clothes that she didn't need to wear the same thing twice for the whole summer. She was loved and spoiled and loved by anyone that had the pleasure of meeting my little angel. So I let her wear her hair out with a flower headband. She looked like a little doll baby. Looking and feeling like a million we go to the hot spot where everyone hangs in the summer, the ice cream parlor on Main Street in Pleasantville. Known for its cheap ice cream, pretty ladies that like to hang around, and its parking lot pimping. Any given day you can see a gang of bikers gathering or a gaggle of pretty women posted up leaning on their freshly washed cars. It was the place to be seen at and the only place to be when it was above 80 degrees around these parts.

Swaying my ass to the invisible music banging in my ears, holding my daughters hand we climb out of our air conditioned car water ice to cool down on this sweltering day. Samya was still a baby, she still only had limited palette. Her favorite flavor was watermelon; my favorite was strawberry. Leaning on the hood of my car while Mina sat savoring the flavors bursting across my tongue, we were just people watching enjoying the day. She was still little but wanted her independence when feeding herself. It was sticky central once she got half way thru and just didn't want to touch the water ice anymore. I was always prepared with a back up outfit for moments just like this. A quick clean up was in order before we hoped in the car and headed home. Standing with the trunk open wiping Samina's arms and face I get that prickly feeling like someone was watching, but not in the "I see you" kind of way. More like a person trying to look into my soul. Looking around I see people out enjoying the weather but not one stands out as the voyeur. Gathering everything up after baby girl made I mess we decided to call it a night. I was ready to go home and relax after being out in the heat all day. Checking my mirrors before I back out the parking space I get that same being watched but I believe I see a familiar face. It was like looking at a blast from my past but older and wiser. Life and age can change a person to either make them look better or worse. Well let me say this, time and life must have been great to Jimmy. He turned and smiled in my direction with a look of recognition that told me the eyes I felt were his. My body was on autopilot and immediately wanted to hug my old friend but my nerves kept me rooted in my seat. In the pit of my stomach I felt butterflies and the all consuming tug of recognition. I definitely knew him; he was that hard to forget.

See me and Jimmy had a class together before I had Samya. The universe put us together before when the timing was terrible and we couldn't really act on it. Late nights studying for this accounting class, we bonded over our mutual hate of math. We never slept together but we did kiss. The chemistry was off the charts but we never took it much farther. It was a good time and good laughs when we got together. Once I realized that he was still hung up on his kid's mother, I let it go. It was pointless, I was still with Los and I loved him without a doubt. It was no point in pursuing a guy that was distracted with his own situation. He was always a gentleman and always treated me with respect. I just believe that it wasn't meant for us to be together seriously at the time. But now 3 years later, after the bull shit with Los, I felt like this was fate shining down on me in my favor. Lying in bed that night I had fanciful thoughts of lying up and laughing with Jimmy. Sleeping with a smile I tried to figure out a way to get in touch with Jimmy, I wanted to see him again.

Mornings are always hectic when you have a toddler who touches everything in sight. After changing Samina clothes twice because she spilled her cup, I couldn't wait to get some caffeine in me. It seemed like I worked a full day in two hours after chasing her around. After dropping baby girl off to the sitter, I decided to get my morning coffee from the local spot. Lo and behold I walked in and bumped straight into the man I couldn't get off my mind all night.

"Wow, I thought I seen you yesterday at the ice cream parlor. I said nah, that can't be Kennedy!" Jimmy says as he leans in to hug me. His frame dwarfed my body, enveloping me in his clean scent. He was dressed like a white collar professional with the fresh line up had him looking like a GQ model. He holds me at arms length and basically just undressed me with his eyes.

"I haven't seen you in years! You look great! I thought you moved out of state?" I said.

"No I moved 45 minutes away a couple of years ago but decided to come back to take care of my mother." Jimmy said.

"I see you have a baby now. Are you married?" he asked.

"Actually, I'm not. I was engaged but I called off the whole thing. You know how life is really funny. You can think you have everything planned out only to be thrown a curve ball. But enough about me, what's up with you?" I asked.

"Nothing single, still only 1 kid, he's 5 years old. Just out here trying to enjoy my life and get paid" he said.

"So you're single Kennedy? You trying go out with me and have a couple of drinks? No pressure."

"I'm something like single. Samina's dad got into some trouble before we met and he just got sentenced and sent up Washington

Township to serve his time. But in the mean and in between I'm not waiting around for anyone." I said.

The light went off behind his eyes that radiated towards me. The universe sends people at the right time and place; because Lawd knows I needed some companionship. And not for nothing, he was like a match to flame. I couldn't get him off my mind after I seen him yesterday. I had it bad and I knew that I wanted him. I knew that I would have him my way on my terms.

"So tomorrow? I'll give you my number; call me in the day time to confirm our plans. I can't wait!" Jimmy said.

He literally eye fucked me and had me naked on the side walk in all of 5 seconds. The familiar pull of arousal that had evaded me came back in waves. Smiling in my direction, I can't help but to take in the whole package. Smooth au lait skin that trail down to toned arms tatted up, warm brown eyes framing a face with perfect teeth off set by dimples so deep you might fall in. I couldn't wait to have adult conversation that didn't revolve around kids and work. Plus it didn't hurt that he was sexy as sin. With the caffeine in hand, I turned and waved as I pulled out my cell to text my best friend.

Me: Aye you busy
Peyton: At work beat, what's up?
Me: Guess who I seen today?
Peyton: Who?
Me: JIMMY!!!!
Peyton: Not Jimmy from before?!?! Gtfoh
Me: Yaaaasssssss Bitch! We were going out tomorrow.
I need you to keep baby girl for me.
Peyton: No problem, let's go to the mall when I get off.
Me: Ok, thanks luv you

For the rest of the day with the excitement and anticipation I was floating. It was like I was rushing the night just so I could wake up and get to my date. The feeling you have when it's all fresh, shiny and new. Peyton picked me up around 6 that night when she got off so we could go to the mall. We made a beeline straight for VS. New panties were in order, even though I knew I had no intentions on sleeping with him that night, the new undergarments on your skin make you feel sexy. And I just wanted to feel better about myself and life in general at that point. I was ready to feel something other than pain or anger.

After several hours of shopping, $400 lighter on my pockets, we were ready to get something to eat. Pulling up a stool in our favorite local seafood spot we order Kettle 1 and Sprite while waiting for a table.

"So what are you gonna wear? You just brought like six dresses! You tryna take it slow or fuck him tomorrow?" Peyton asked as she looked over the rim of the glass taking a sip.

"I really want to just fuck him but I don't want him to think I just want him for sex or vice versa. We already knew each other from before and never had sex! I literally was too drunk and he was too much of a gentleman. When I finally woke up fully clothed like "Hey, did we? You know!" He said he felt like that was taking advantage of me because I was drunk. How chivalrous?" I said.

"Well wear the green dress that laces up the back. Ohhh, with silver sandals with gold jewelry! Carry your little clutch to tie the whole outfit together. You'll look sexy enough to bite but not like you ready to just take the dress off as soon as he picks you up!" Peyton said.

"I agree I want to look hot enough that he wants to touch me, but too nice that he's afraid to touch me in fear of ruining my outfit!" I said.

We high fived just as our buzzer beeped alert us to our waiting table being available so we can eat. The conversation and drinks kept flowing keeping us in a celebratory mood. Hopping back in her car to get dropped off at home, blasting Camron we sang along extra loud. Pulling up in front of my house she popped the trunk so I could my bags. Hanging out the window Peyton says, "I'll see you tomorrow to pick up baby girl. Get some rest and get cute on him!"

As I walked in my house the emotions ranging through me ranged from excited to nervous. Throwing my bags in the closet, I laid back on my bed savoring the fresh smell of vanilla wafting up from the sheets. Running my hands over my breast I feel my nipples peak instantly making my whole inside clench. The anticipation of possible getting it on with Jimmy tomorrow has me wanting to touch myself. Yanking my jeans, I start touching myself through the panties. Panties moisten from the essence of my flower budding from the course texture of the undergarment rubbing back and forth. A moan escapes from between my lips as I rub faster and faster. The friction is so delicious but not enough to crest over the peak. Yanking my panties to the side I thrust one finger in slowly, then two. Savoring the slickness of myself in feel the orgasm rips through me. My whole body convulses as I pictured Jimmy between my legs licking my sensitive nub.

Once the tremors subside enough that I can walk without falling, I shower away the day. Slipping in between my sheets naked, sleep came easy after that orgasm. All I could think is I can't wait to see Jimmy tomorrow.

· · · · · · · · ● · · · · · · · ·

As the sunlight peaks over the horizon casting a glow across my ceiling I smile as I hear baby girl in her room playing. Brushing my teeth, I take stock of the woman in the mirror. Young, supple body, kind smiling eyes, long and lean like a model. I can't fathom why Los would do me so wrong. Staring in the mirror I get flashbacks of all the great times we had. How he helped me become the fantastic mother and home maker that I am. How on cold nights he would heat my towel I the shower before I got out. Or how when I was feeling down he would do this dumb dance just to get me to laugh and put a smile on my face. I thought I seen forever with him. I thought he was my happily ever after, my now and forever. But now I see that it was all a ploy to get what he wanted. A good girl to hold him down but he wanted the chicks in the street. "Well GOOD LUCK with that!" I yelled at the mirror.

"Hey mama's baby! You ready for some breakfast and cartoons? Then we'll get dressed and go to the park. You're staying with Auntie Peyton tonight so mommy can go be an adult." I said to Samya. Looking into her baby face all I could see was her father's features. His eyes, nose, and smile just dominate her features making her a girl replica of him. Sometimes it makes me sad when she does a gesture or moves the way that he used, but he gave me the best gift when he gave me her.

The day was gorgeous. Blue cloudless sky had us running from slides to swings. This little girl had more energy than 10 of me! What a feeling to watch her in all her child wonderment and think that life couldn't get easier for her. I loved her with all of me and to see her happy was like a breath of fresh air. After me and Samya played until almost lunch time, it was time to start getting ready for my meet up.

Peyton came and picked Samya up around 3pm to give enough time to get my life in order before my date. Laying out my outfit for the night, I decided to pair the lace up green halter top with blue skinnies, and green lace up sandals. My hair was still straight from my salon appointment earlier in the week. It was easy to let the soft silky waves falling down my exposed back. Gold polish to accent my nails and toes followed by dark smoky eye makeup with super glossy lips completed the look. Just as I was admiring my handy work, watching myself in the floor length mirror in my living room, I heard a knock at the door. I grab my Versace Red Jeans and spritz the important parts that make the perfume all that more potent when we were in close corners. Grabbing my clutch I ran downstairs to open the door.

Jimmy stood there dressed in linen shirt and pants. Crisp Al's with a fitted cap turned to the side. As soon as leaned in to hug me his scent made my body does involuntary things and reminded of all of our late nights studying together. Kissing my cheek while touching my skin he steps back and looks at me, "Damn, I forgot how you look all dressed up. Let's go before we don't make it to dinner and end up staying here. "Walking hand in hand he opens the car door for me. The electricity flowing between us was magnetic. Checking out the interior of his brand new Audi I was impressed with its opulence. My mind still couldn't wrap around the fact that after all these years that I'm actually going on a date with Jimmy after all the time I fantasized about being with him.

Driving thru downtown with the sunroof open, the breeze so soft caressing my skin as we drive, it was a perfect night to be out. The sky was clear with the moon hanging low and stars shining bright. The sensual voice of R Kelly playing low on his Bose speakers had me feeling some type of way before we even did anything. I could see what he was doing, seducing me without touching. This is the first guy that realized that foreplay starts long before we hit the bedroom. He was definitely aiming for something, I just didn't know if we were on the same page yet.

"I have the perfect place for dinner. If you don't mind I'd like to take you to a lounge later. Is that ok?" he said. "I would love that! It's just so good to be out and about. Thanks for the invite." I said as I leaned over and touched his arm. "Keep touching me and we won't make it to dinner. I'll park somewhere dark and do wicked things to your body." He whispered in my ear. Instantly thoughts of forgetting about dinner and skipping to desert entered my mind. With those words whispered in my ear, I knew that it was highly likely that it would go down between us. But I decided I was going to do it my way, when I was really ready. "I'll remember you offered. But you know skinny girls love to eat!" I said. Sitting back relaxing into the soft leather seats the anticipation of the night had me wound tight. I couldn't wait to see what the night had in store for me if he already had me creaming myself and he never even touched me.

All through dinner the conversation was light and comfortable. Jimmy always had a sense of humor that could rival any comedian, and it didn't hurt that he was extra easy on the eyes. The alcohol kept flowing and so did the laughs. By the time we arrived at the lounge I was ready to hear some mellow music and have a couple more drinks. Grabbing a corner table that was candle lit he order a bottle of champagne. Swaying in my seat I was zoning to the soothing sounds of a Mary J Blige cover. He grabbed my hand and kissed the inside of my wrist, making my stomach flutter at the gesture. "I just wanted to say thank you for allowing me to have the pleasure of entertaining you tonight. I would love to do this again." he said. Instead of replying, I stood from the table still holding his hand. I pulled him to the dance floor with my back to his front. I wrapped his arms around my waist and just swayed with the beat. The heat between or bodies and the liquor had me hotter than fire hot coal. Grinding my hips into his, I can tell that he is just as turned on as I was. Licking my earlobe I sighed as he whispered, "I've been watching you all night and I can't take my eyes off you. I'm trying to be a patient man, but we have history and unfinished business. I want to do some things to you, but I'll wait until the right time. Let's just enjoy each other's company." That's when I just leaned over at the waist and winded my ass on his dick. Slow circles until I turned around and faced. Hands on my waist I looked in his eyes and I could see the desire brimming over. There were no words that needed to be spoken between us; it was so obvious that even a blind man could see that we had a thing for each other.

He grabbed my hand as we walked back to our table to clear up the bill. I excused myself so I could freshen up in the bathroom before we left the lounge. Looking at my reflection as I washed my hands I couldn't believe the face staring back at me was I. This woman in the mirror was sexy, hair softly messy from dancing, cheeks flushed from the excitement and eyes shiny with the promise of good things to come.

Touching up my lipstick and spraying a spritz of perfume between my breasts, I walked out the bathroom looking more composed than I felt. He undressed me with his eyes as I sauntered back over to the table. He was looking at me like a starved man and I was a buffet. His look of being enamored with me just made my walk get meaner to give him a show. Walking out to valet his car arrived as soon as I we stood on the curb. I slide into the passenger seat and got comfortable for the short ride back to my house. Even though it was late, I never wanted the night to end. This is the first time in years that I didn't have anxiety or guilt hanging over my head making me worry about every single move that I made. "Can I take you somewhere before I take you home?" he asked while his hand made circles on my thigh. "Sure!" I beamed at him. We pulled up to a local make out spot overlooking the water. Getting out the car he grabbed a blanket from his trunk and spread it on the hood. Sitting on the hood he grabbed my feet and gently laid them on his lap. Taking off the shoes he rubbed my feet and caressed my calf. His hard strong hands worked my muscles into putty. The right amount of pain with pleasure had a moan escaped from between my lips. All I could think was he had magic hands. We just sat there with him rubbing my feet and me watching the waves. A peaceful silence had fallen over us; there were no need for words for what was already understood. He just looks over at me and watches my face as the look of euphoria covers my face from what he was doing to my feet and legs. "I just wanted to spend more time with you before I had to take you home. I really enjoyed myself and I hope that you give me a chance again to spend some time with you. But it's getting late, let me get you home. And I have an early morning tomorrow. If I don't get you home soon, you know!" He said putting my shoes back on strapping them up. He grabbed my hand and pulled me off the hood walking me back to the passenger side of the car. Putting away the blanket he got in a headed toward my house. His hand was warm in mine as we pulled up in front he led me to the front door. Butterflies danced in my belly thinking on how to proceed after the night that we had. "Jimmy, I had......" was all I got out before he smashed me to the front door and kissed me hard. From the moment his lips touched mine it was like an electrical current running between us like being zapped and melded together seamlessly. I had never felt like that from a kiss, like I could cum on the spot. Eyes closed panting while he assaulted my mouth, when he pulled back I was breathless, even a lil light headed. "Till next time sweetheart." Jimmy said while backing down the steps to his car. Standing in my door way I was flushed, horny, and happy. Fucking Jimmy, I couldn't believe it! We should have been did that! I was thirsty for attention and time, everything this one night with him was giving me. I was thirsty for him.

Late nights spent talking on the phone until we asleep, teenage ish. The thing is I was so sexually attracted to him that all I could think about when we were together was about riding his dick. But he was being stingy, making me work for it. Wining and dining me, rubbing me, caressing me, never in the sexual way but anyway that he touched me felt like a thousand deaths. I was getting frustrated; it was only so many times touching yourself imagining that your hands are his can get you off. I wanted the real thing, I wanted his dick bad. Since being a lady had me waiting on him to make a move, I decided that it would be better if I was proactive about cumming. I mean if he wasn't going to make a move on me, I would make him into fucking me.

After weeks of hanging out, I decided that I would just seduce him. That morning I called him and invited him over after work. I told him I would cook and we could watch a movie. Samya was with her grandma so I had the whole house to myself. Once he agreed, I made it my mission to have everything in place so that my plan would go off without a hitch.

Marinating some steaks in the fridge, I cut up the veggies to make a salad and a couple of potatoes to roast. Cleaning my house from top to bottom making everything shine, lit scented candles glowing lightly giving off a romantic ambiance, all that was left was for me to get myself together. Taking a long shower with scented soaps, I shaved, scrubbed and exfoliated until my skin was soft as a feather. I had the slow jams pumping through the hidden speakers all over the house putting me in the seductive state of mind. Rubbing sweet coconut oil into my skin I wanted to smell just as good as I tasted. Throwing on a maxi dress that brushed the floor when I walked, I put my hair in a messy bun and just a touch of lip gloss to complete my laid back sexy look. I danced through the kitchen finishing prepping the food since he was due to arrive in an hour. That gave me ample time to be hot and ready for the night ahead. But before I could even flip the steaks he was knocking on the door.

Sashaying over to the door, I did a quick scan to make sure everything was in place. Two wine glasses sat in the middle of the table with a bottle of red wine complimented by little finger foods that can be feed to each other. Jimmy walks in and kisses me on my cheek carrying a bottle of vodka.

"I know how you like your vodka, but I can see you already have everything in motion." He said glancing around the dimly light living area. I could tell that the scent of marinated meat was assaulted his senses the way he put his head back and inhaled.

"Do you have a drink preference, because I set out wine? We can do some shots, I'm down." I said.

"It's up to you sexy. Whatever you want, I want to give it to you."

"Nah you don't want what I want, cause if you did you would have been taken advantage of me all these times we have been in private together."

"That's exactly why I'm waiting, because once we go to that point, there is no coming back." Jimmy said as he pressed his front to me. I felt bold, bold enough to take my hand and trace it over the bulge in his pants.

"Maybe I don't want to come back. Maybe I want you to take me over the edge." I said in a husky voice as I undid his belt buckle letting his pants fall to the floor.

"So you just go to let the food burn?"

"I would rather have something else in my mouth beside steak." getting on my knees looking up at him. Licking my lips I yanked his jeans and underwear down. One of the most beautiful brown cocks that I ever seen sprang free and stood at attention. Looking him in the eye I circled the head of his dick with my tongue. Closing my eyes savoring the taste and feel that is uniquely him, the eroticism of the act made me moan. Cupping his balls as he pumped into my mouth, I watched his face to see his reaction. His mouth parted and he sighed as we made eye contact. Watching me hollowing out my cheeks trying to swallow his whole dick like it was my last meal. I was so turned on it was impossible for me not to try to relieve the yearning in the pit of my stomach. I had to touch myself. Reaching my hand in between my legs I could feel the wetness coating my fingers. The sensation was so great I had to close my eyes to be able to focus on how my senses were heightened. The more I sucked the more turned on I became. Moaning over his dick, I could feel the first trickle of awareness trying to release itself from my body. And just when I thought he would blow, he stopped me.

"You have on too many clothes, take that dress off." He said as he stroked himself. I stood and turned my back to him. Looking over my shoulder as I slowly lifted the dress over my head revealing the lace thong that I had on. I was grateful that I had the fore sight to not where a bra. My nipples pebbled as they became exposed to the cool temperature in the house. Turning to face him, I dropped my hands revealing my soft supple breast to him. He didn't know what to look at first, me as the whole pie, or my breast being exposed naked to eyes for the first time ever. None of that mattered because I could tell by the look of desire on his face, that he was about to devour me whole. That look caused a fresh wave of moisture drenched my pussy.

"If I would have known that you looked like that underneath those clothes I would have been tried to get you naked."

"If I knew you tasted so good, I would have been put you in my mouth." I said licking my bruised lips.

He grabbed my waist and pulled me flush against his body kissing me hard. Hands caressing and grabbing like he had was an octopus. Every place that he touched felt like it was fire kissing my skin. I was so turned on I couldn't wait to feel him on top of me, but he had other plans.

"Sit on the table and lay back. Let me worship this body that I have admired from a far but could never touch." he said. Lying back with my feet flat on the table, he slowly rubbed up my legs getting closer and closer to the spot that I wanted him to touch for so long. But he wanted to draw it out as long as possible. He wanted to tease me until I begged him to fuck me, but I wasn't going to break. I had the resolve of the secret service men, he would beg me first. Kissing up my thighs a moan slipped out of my puffy lips making me want to wrap my legs around his neck.

"Tell me Kennedy, what do you want me to do to you? You want me to taste this kitty? What Kennedy? Tell me!" All the while kissing my inner thighs murmur sweet nothings into my skin.

"I want you to taste her, lick her. I want you in me, over me. Just don't stop! Please!" I begged.

Jimmy grunted has he pulled my body to the end of the table so he could sit down and feast. I felt his breath before his lips kissed my clit. Instead of him going right for my sweet spot, he kissed and licked everything except where I wanted him to be. I felt insane with lust for him. When his lips finally covered that spot, my back arched as he licked and nibbled my pussy. He gave me wet sloppy head that had a puddle on my dining room table from him going so hard on me. Watching my expression as he had his face between my thighs he seen me trying to hide the look of utter pleasure from my face. Just when

I thought I couldn't take anymore the damn burst. My soul damn near levitated from the release of pent up anticipation. Moaning while grinding his face into my clit, I pinched my nipples making the orgasm rip through my small frame. The predatory look he gave me let me know that everything that I imagined the last couple of weeks was about to go down! Standing up he grabbed my ankles and put them over his shoulders fucking me with his eyes the whole time. Grabbing a condom he placed on the table, he sheathed himself still watching me. Rubbing the head in circles building the tension back up so fast, I almost forgot that he made me cum less than five minutes.

"Please!" I begged.

"Please what Kennedy?"

"Please Jimmy; fuck the shit out of me!" I moaned out.

He thrust into me filling me all the way to the hilt. Both of us overwhelmed by the sensation created when our bodies met. Can you envision me on my back on the dining room table, naked? He was standing between my golden thighs, with this look of determination on his face as he tried to keep his composure from ruining the moment? Legs spread waiting for him to stroke us both over the edge of no return? We were so in tuned with each other that our movements were like a dance. Two bodies joining as one, making lust feel like love. Then I felt like I couldn't take anymore, I had lights behind my eyes each time he thrust into me. Just when I felt my whole core tighten, and I screamed out "I'm cumming!" his movements became jerky. I rode the wave and became unhinged until we both fell over the edge clinging on to each other like a life raft. And that's how the beginning became the end. This is how I started my downward spiral of deceit and lies. With another dude between my thighs, making me forget that I had a man already.

CHAPTER 3
The Falling

Three months. Three months of us becoming more than friends less than a relationship. Three months of us double dating. Three months of laughs, fun in the sun, drunken club nights, followed by fucking until the sun came up. He did things to my body that I had only imagined. Things that when you think about them you automatically blush and remember the feeling you felt. We spent endless nights up smoking that Loud, watching movies talking about life. It was unspoken about a relationship but we had started making plans for the future. Mini vacations, local shows that were coming up that we both wanted to see. It felt good; it felt right to be with him, easy. I just really enjoyed the fact that he accepted me, for me. Not Kennedy the mom, Kennedy the woman. Even though I didn't give him a chance to interact with my daughter that much, he still always included her in anything he did. Always bringing her little gifts and inquiring about what was going on with us. He was interested in my life and what I had going on. He was interested in anything that had to do with me. And I was enthralled to have him.

As the summer wound down and we got closer to time for Los to come home, I started to get anxiety. It was two folds, about this guy coming home with unresolved issues between us. I hadn't spoken to him or written him since he went away. I also knew that Los would resent me because he felt like I left him and moved on without him. The thing is my heart was still Los'. It was fun to be with another guy who seen me, but the love I had for Los never dimmed. Jimmy never fit into my real life; you know the building a life together. Carlos was the father of my daughter and I would do everything to give her the father that I never had ever. Jimmy was a vacation and a fantasy wrapped in one. Days spent with him blowing stacks on me and Peyton, just to get me home and take me to another planet. He wasn't ready for a real relationship that entailed him being a part of my world. He liked the trussed up and painted girl with the smart mouth and quick wit. He didn't know my fears and goals. He never met my family, had never picked my daughter up from daycare. I only revealed myself to him in the best light, always flawless. I let him get a glimpse into my life, a bird's eye view, all superficial. Jimmy got to see what I wanted him to see. It was all infatuation on my behalf and what ifs. I was in love with the idea of everyday being like how we spent the summer. It was all a façade, because in real life you share your problems with your significant other. But we were so vain in our lust, it never got that deep. Like I said I had bigger problems, Los was coming home and I was still trying to figure out how to get back to how things were before everything went wrong. Jimmy might have known my body better than me, but he didn't know my heart better than Carlos. Because if he did he would have known what was about to happen before I even had to open mouth. He would have seen the signs before it got to that point. Don't get me wrong, I loved them both, but in two different ways. And the love that I felt for the man I dedicated the last couple years of my life was greater. But I stilled loved him, and I wanted things to work out for us. It was time to tell Jimmy that our affair was over and I was nervous.

That night Jimmy, Manny, Peyton, and I went on one of usual night excursions of food, drinks, music, and weed. Every chance we got we all linked and partied like there was no tomorrow. Me and Jimmy up all night in the bar flirting with each other like we never met. We danced close like lovers just reunited after a long business trip. He rocked me in his arms while I grinded back into him trying to make two bodies become one. No words just all action as I wound around him like it was just us on the dance floor. I think he knew that this was our last hurrah because he held me tight like he would never let me go. I just wanted him to know that this was more than a fling for me; I was highly infatuated with him. I could love him if I had more time, but I loved Los without a fault. So I loved Jimmy the best way I knew how, and I hoped that he understood.

Leaving from the bar after last call he drove me home. We both rode in comfortable both lost in our own thoughts. The silence was so complete that even the low hum of the tires on the road didn't make a difference. Confliction in my heart had me debating on telling him now or telling him later. Should I let him make love to me not knowing that this would be the last time? Or should I tell him now know that I would never feel the warmth of his embrace every again? Staring out the window, I was lost in my own mind until he reached over and caressed my hand kissing each finger as he navigated towards my neighborhood. The fire started to burn where he his lips touched, the sparks radiating to my pussy. Between the alcohol and dancing I was already turned all the way on. One good fuck for the road I thought, just enough to have that memory in my mind to last a lifetime. Pulling into my driveway I hopped out pulling my skirt over my thighs, I could barely open the door. The feelings swirling around in me had me disorientated, my mind was trying to compartmentalize where what feelings belonged. The wetness between my thighs made my legs stick together. In my mind's eye, I could see exactly what was about to happen. It made my palms sweaty and my legs weak. Keys dropping on the floor from my hands shaking so bad, thinking this would be the last time we would be together like this. After tonight we would be strangers again, pretending that he last 3 months never happened. Jimmy would be somebody that I used to know.

Busting through the door giggling as he groped me as he pushed the door closed. I wanted him twice as bad as he wanted me. My emotions were on overload from the thought of not being able to see him again, his out of pure lust for the moment we were about to share. Hoisting me onto his waist, I gave him my tongue. I put all the words that I would never say into that kiss. Kissing like he was my oxygen and I couldn't breathe without his lips covering mine. Lost in the heat of our exchange, time stood still and gave us space to do us. We tumbled onto the bed, his hands lifting my skirt to touch me. Panties so wet that they stuck to my body, the friction making me wetter by the second. This wasn't going to be making love; this was us satisfying our own urges in a carnal type of way. Pulling my panties off Jimmy fucked me with all my clothes on. Skirt hiked up to my waist, shirt pulled down exposing my nipples, high heels over his shoulders. All you could hear was skin touch skin and me moaning every time he almost pulled all the way out and thrust with so much force that he was hitting the bottom with every stroke. He fucked me hard like he knew that this was it for us. Then he turned hard into soft and sensual making my body want to weep for release. He had me so wound up that I thought that at any second I would shatter. He stroked my body over and over till the sensations all blended together into one huge bundle of nerves hovering over my orgasm threatening to push us both over the edge way too fast. Kissing my neck and shoulders was the last thing I remember before the light behind my eyes burst and in a gush I came all wet and sloppy all over his dick. The wetness that dripped down my thighs made his movements jerky like he was losing control. With him filling me all the way up he kissed me without moving. We both knew that it was a ploy to keep this round going. It didn't make me mad that I made him come undone; he had been doing that to me since we had been fucking. As I was coming down off my high, I had the overwhelming urge to show him through my movements that I had a real thing for him, not just someone to fill my time. Pushing him on his back, I got on top. Instead of going for broke, I took my time. Kissing him from neck to navel, soft nips that made him jump with every touch. I could tell that it was taking all his self control to keep from cumming before I put it back in. I eased down onto his cock slowly, an inch at a time, swirling every time I came back up. Winding my hips, round and round, up and down, then I would stop. I became a sex goddess, wanton in nature but completely in control of what I was doing to his body. Riding him slow to build the tension up, holding his hands above his hands I fucked Jimmy. I kissed his mouth and said freaky shit in his ear about how he was making me feel. He moaned that I was going to kill him. That it was too good this time. Grabbing my waist taking control he pounded me.

I nipped his ear as I felt my walls convulsing around his dick and said to him "I'm going to cum Jimmy, cum with me!" He didn't say anything just grunted and kept up the pace as he ground against my clit. His dick pulsed in time to my walls clenching, we were going to come at the same time.

Just as my 2nd orgasm ripped through me, he came too. Long spurts of hot cum pumped into the condom just as I was coming down. Lying in the bed after the performance I started to feel guilty. Guilt that I mislead Jimmy into fucking me again without knowing that it was going to be the last time. The guilt of Los would find out about Jimmy before I had a chance to tell him myself. Guilt that I knew nothing was ever going to be the same again.

My legs threatened to give out on me, so I just curled up with him next to the table we almost broke. With labored breathing, it was a clarity moment. It was now or never to reveal the truth to him. It wasn't that I was scared of losing him, I never any intentions on carrying on this affair once Los came home. That just wasn't how I moved and I knew that being sneaky can cause other problems that lead to worse problems. Watching crime TV made you aware of just how often love triangles end in despair. I didn't want to be a victim from being shady; everyone in the situation had the right to know what position they played. Even if they felt like they've been wronged my conscious would be clear.

"I have to tell you something." I said

"What?" Jimmy said as he snuggled closer to me.

"Before I tell you, I want you to know that everything between us was real. I enjoy every moment we share and I appreciate the love and attention you have given me. The last couple of months have been heaven sent. You and I has been everything that I hoped and imagined it could be."

He leaned onto his elbow and looked at me, I could tell he was wondering where I was going with this. Instead of saying anything he just looked at me waiting for me to tell him what had me all emotional and shut off at the same time all of a sudden. The words tasted like lead as the tears tried to escape from the corner of my eyes. Wiping them away quickly, I took a breather before I told him.

"My daughter's father gets released tomorrow from prison. We have unfinished business. I need to see this through for the sake of my child and my own curiosity. I never wanted to hurt you, but you came to me at the perfect time to ease my mind. I feel terrible to tell you this way, but you had a right to know." I pleaded.

He just looked at me, grabbed his clothes and went in the bathroom. A couple of seconds later I hear the water running. Sitting there on my bed, I hoped that I was making the right decision by not moving on and sticking with Los.

Jimmy walked out of the bathroom fully dressed and grabbed his keys. Walking towards the door he turned and said "its cool Kennedy, I like you. Not enough to deal with the drama your about to start. You could have been told me, but you just think about yourself. You had me thinking that this was going somewhere, but now I see that it was just something to pass the time. I hope everything works out for you." And just like that he walked out of my life.

● ● ● ● ● ● ● ● ● ⬤ ● ● ● ● ● ● ● ● ●

"Come on Samya, daddy will be coming out those doors right there!" I said to my daughter a couple hours after I had just been in the bed with another man. We were in front of the gates of Hell waiting for Los to be released. I tried to keep up appearances but the love that I once had for him changed. They say that absence makes the heart grow fonder; well in this case it made my heart turn colder. Even though I tried to convince myself that we could get back tight, my mind wouldn't let me believe that. The damage and betrayal had already happened. Now I had a whole relationship with someone else and my heart was mended by Jimmy where Carlos had broken it. My feelings were still hurt by his betrayal and I just wanted everything to be like how it was before all this. As Samya toddled around the car I see the gate open and him walk out. Prison had been good to him; working out every day had brought back the guy I first met. Running thru the gates he picked us both up and hugged us.

"Look at Daddy's pretty girl! All big dressed up waiting for me! And look at Daddy's big girl looking sexy as the day I met her!" Los said hugging me close to his chest. I was rigid, my posture was tight because I knew that once we were alone, all the animosity I had in me would boiling over and burn him.

"Let's get out of here and get on the road. Take you back to the house so you shower and change. You hungry, let's eat first." I said as we walked hand and hand back to the car. His hand felt good in mine, but it wasn't how it used to feel. The spark that usually accompanied his hand touching mine wasn't there. Putting baby girl in her car seat we hoped on the road to get back home. It was going to take a while to get adjusted to him being back in my lives.

Having Los back put me at ease somewhat after months of budgeting. It felt good to have money to spend on myself and Mina without worrying if I would be able to afford to live on. See he was always a great father and excellent provider, but a sucky ass significant other. He never took my needs as a woman into account to make our relationship stronger or better. No gifts just because or night outs just to celebrate our love. It was like all he cared about was the money, his daughter, and keeping me whether I was happy or satisfied. The streets had changed in the time that he left and came back. Dudes that were supposed to show loyalty, switched up. People that owed him money disappeared. The spot where he hustled out of got raided, so there wasn't any flow. That's how we ended up pulling a heist. See even when you do things under the cloak of night, people are still watching. And here I thought I was being discreet only to overlook the fact that my neighbors are nosey. So they tell Los that they seen some guy coming and going in the dark while he was locked away. After hours and hours of arguing I finally confessed. That yes I was seeing someone while he was I away. The whole situation had me aggy, because it wasn't that I wasn't going to tell him. I wanted to tell him on my own time. It wasn't a secret that I wanted to carry or have in my heart knowing that I was blatantly deceptive. I was hurting and lonely. I needed some attention, the attention I was missing while he was home that felt like we had a whole country between us when he went away. I believed that Carlos and I were over forever. But after listening to Samya cry over her Papa, I knew that I had to at least attempt to make it work for her.

He questioned my loyalty to our family and gave me an ultimatum. He wanted to set Jimmy up to be robbed. He knew that he was getting a little coin and figured this was his easiest come up. Of course I was against the idea; I never wanted to hurt Jimmy. All Jimmy wanted to do was love me, never hurt me. But I knew that if I didn't agree the consequences that followed wouldn't be good for me and Mina. Going back and forth with him was a dead issue; he already had the idea in his head and was sticking to it. Carlos had never shown me his violent side in all the time we had been together, but now I could see that he kept that side of his personality a secret from me. He had me terrified of what he was capable of doing especially since he felt like he had a personal vendetta against the guy I was seeing. He never put his hands on me but he would verbally crush me with every opportunity that he had. The weight of that alone was enough that I didn't want to be in the way of his wrath. So after being emotionally starved and verbally abused, I caved under the pressure.

"Look either you with it or not. Either way, he's done. It's no way he gets to walk around here knowing he fucked my girl and still looking flossy." Los said pacing around the bedroom we shared.

"It's not that Los, I want to help you. I just don't want it to come back on me and the baby. You're mad at him, but you should be mad at him. I agreed to date him knowing we were just going through something. He would have never pursued me if he knew that you were still in the picture." I said with my eyes averted.

"Why are you defending him? You love him or something? You want to be with him? You think you going to take my daughter and be a happy family with him? THAT would never happen! I will kill him first"

"Why would say that? If I wanted him, I would be with him! I'm here with you, trying to figure out how you trying to go back to jail, away from your daughter again indefinitely."

"Quiet all that noise you talking! Since you want to be fucking this dude, I need him to pay me! You belong to me, and since you want to be a whore he needs to pay your pimp!" he yelled.

"I was never a whore, and you were never my pimp! If you feel the need to take what that man worked for be my guest. But please leave me out of it." I pleaded.

"Leave you out of it? You fucked him in our house! Where our daughter lives? You created this!" spreading his arms while he spun around the bedroom.

"Why do you want to rob him? You have more than enough, and you make more money than he ever can!"

"So you love this clown? You want to protect him? Yeah I make more money but I want all he has for trying to destroy what we had!"

"This is stupid and dangerous! But if this is what it takes, I will do it! If doing this makes you happy, I'll do it!" I wailed as tears streamed down my face.

"Good, I'm happy you see things this my way. So here's the plan. You tell him you want to talk to him. Go to house in one of those slinky dresses that you like to wear. Take this bottle of Henny with you. Offer him a drink then put this powder in his drink. It only takes about 5 minutes before he passes out. Then you call me and I'll be parked up the street from his house. All you gotta do is act like you miss him, which shouldn't be hard considering you really do miss his bitch ass. I'm taking all his shit! Call him now!" Los said as he paced back and forth.

"So you already had this planned out? How?"

"Don't worry about it, just do what I tell you and everything will go off without a hitch."

Grabbing my cell, I looked through my contact until I found his number. I hadn't talk to him in over a month since he walked out of my front door without a backwards glance. For all I know he changed his number or just wasn't beat to talk to me. The way things ended wasn't on the best of terms. He didn't even give me a chance to try to explain everything. This call could go either way, but I had a feeling that he still had a thing for me.

Me: Hey Jimmy, its Kennedy. I miss you.

Him: (sighs) Really, Kennedy? I haven't heard from you since your daughter's father came home. It wouldn't be soon enough if I never heard from you again. You hurt me and I'm not beat for the bull shit. What do you want?

Me: I want to see you, apologize. I just got out the shower and had this bottle. I wanted to have a drink with you. Do you mind if I came over?

Him: (sighs) I guess, just for a minute though. Call me when you're on your way.

Me: Ok give me 20 minutes.

Hanging up I look over at Los and all I can see is the rage in his eyes. It frightened me that he could be that angry over something that he asked me to do. Grabbing my arm he yanked me up the stairs. "Get dressed so we can do this." Slinging me on the bed I started putting on my clothes. He stood in the corner and watched me as I dressed and applied my makeup. "Oh, you really are going all out for this guy! Just wait and see what happens!" he taunted. As I hurriedly dressed I was trying to figure out how to get out of this situation. I couldn't go through with his plan without someone getting hurt. He wanted me to commit a felony on another street dude that was just as affiliated as he was. He wanted me to set someone up who didn't do anything but try to love me. If Carlos loved me, he wouldn't ask me to be involved in this fuckery like I was a common hood girl with nothing to lose. I was supposed to be his future wife and he wanted me to risk my life, which would also affect our daughter's life. I was torn between my lover and child's father. It had to be a happy medium that I didn't think of yet. It didn't matter because I was running out of time to find a solution. The way Los was staring at me, he knew I was trying to figure it all out, but he would have none of that. It was his way or the highway.

After I got dressed Carlos handed me a small envelope that had the crushed sleeping pill in it.

"Maybe we shouldn't do this, I have a bad feeling." I said before I got in my car.

"Listen, I heard enough of what you think and feel. Either your with the shits or not. If you're not with it we got a serious problem, so you better be with it." Carlos said holding my car door open so that I couldn't drive off. The look on his face was something out of a Thriller movie; he looked nothing like the man that knew. Shutting the car door, I just kept my mouth shut out of fear that whatever I said would set him off. I didn't want to be at the brunt of his anger so I just followed his lead.

The whole way to his house I kept checking the rear view mirror hoping I wouldn't see Carlos's menacing gaze when I looked back. That was a short lived dream since because he followed the whole way and parked a half of block from Jimmy's house. Cutting the engine, I wiped my sweaty palms on my jeans. I walked up his driveway with the bottle in hand and tried not to look so nervous but I could sense the impending doom on the horizon. He greeted me at the door before I could even knock with a smile on his face. I tried to smile but it came across as grimace. Looking into his eyes he must have noticed the look of apprehension as I crossed the threshold. I was shivering even though it was 80 degrees outside; the cold was coming from my soul. Goosebumps rose on my arms as he leaned in and hugged me.

"What's wrong?" he asked me.

I couldn't do it. I couldn't let Jimmy walk into an ambush that I set up. Los was crazy and irrational in his plan and I refused to be a part of it. Jimmy gave me an out by asking me what's wrong.

"He wants me to set you up! He's outside waiting for me to drug you and storm in here and rob you! I couldn't allow that knowing that you never did anything to him. He's mad because he thinks that I love you and that you are a distraction on us being happy. But it's not you, he's crazy! I don't know what to do!" I cried as fell to my knees.

"Shhhsh! Don't worry! I'm always prepared when people think they are going to rob me! Call him, tell him I took the drink and you're in the bathroom." He said going to his cabinet pulling out a loaded .22. Cocking the chamber he checked to make sure it was fully loaded.

"You do know it's either him or me. I plan on it being his day." he said calmly looking at me.

"I know, but that is Samina's dad! Please there has to be another way! My daughter won't have a father if you this goes left! I don't want that on my conscience! I might be afraid but I don't hate him. I don't want to see him or you hurt!"

"He should have thought of that before he decided to use you to set me up! Now go in the bathroom and call him!"

It seemed like whatever I did, it still ended the same way. Someone was going to get hurt, and all of it was because of me. Not because I deceived anyone, or lied. I was nothing but honest and both of these guys wanted to be the bigger man. I wanted to tell them both that it was choice to do what I did. It had nothing to do with either one of them and the outcome of this situation wouldn't sway me in any direction.

Sulking into the bathroom I text him:

> Me: He took the drink, I'm in the bathroom.
> The backdoor is unlocked
> Carlos: Ok, stay in the bathroom
> Me: Ok

Sitting on the sink I hung my head at the situation that I was in. My baby dad had a vendetta on my joint. He wanted him hurt because he felt like that's what came in between us, not his ways. I start thinking back to all the good times me Los and I had, the time before we had Samya. When everything was till good and we didn't have any problems. When I knew that he loved me unconditionally without fault. How when I had Samya he cried as he held her the first time. Or how he would make love to me all night long until I couldn't stand it. Then I thought about Jimmy. I knew him longer than I knew Los but we just connected on an emotional level recently. About all the summer nights we spent laying up drinking and partying. I was thankful for both of them and the dynamics they brought to my life. I never expected it to be a Wild Wild West showdown over me. The tears just flowed as these thoughts swirled around my head. Snapping out of my daydream I heard a gunshot, and a scream that could pierce the walls. Followed by a scuffle and several different gunshots in rapid succession letting me know that whatever was happening was over. Waiting for the noise to die down I walked into the living room to see Los sprawled out on the couch, with blood pouring from his stomach and bubbling from between his lips. A dark puddle was spreading from under his body and trickled down onto the floor. Jimmy was laid out between the living room and the dining area. The blood seeping from under his body reminded me of an upscale area rug. It smelled like gun powder and death. Red was the color of the day because everything was splattered in it. Staring at the scene in horror, I didn't know whether to run, scream, or call 911.

Running to check Carlos's pulse I didn't feel anything. It was too late for him to continue his mental reign of terror. Just when I was getting ready to check Jimmy's pulse he started moaning. With 2 gunshot wounds too, one in his thigh on in his arm, he was still alive and pissed off.

"His bitch ass came into my house and wanted to murder me?! MURDER ME?! Fuck out of here with that shit!" He wheezed out.

"Shhhhsh, don't talk!"

"Call 911! I'm bleeding to death!" he said as he passed out again.

At that moment the weight of what happened started to dawn on me. I went into self preservation mode and tried to figure out the best course of action that didn't involve me getting in trouble. These two men wouldn't have known or cared about each other. I was the common denominator. Many a wars had been started for centuries over women and I just started one. My lover killed my father's daughter while I was in the other room. I knew that I was mostly responsible for what transpired but I refused to acknowledge that fact. I tried to stop this before it even started but the egos of two alpha males got the best of me. Running into the bathroom I flushed the powder Los had given me to drug Jimmy. Grabbing his cell I deleted the messages that we had sent between us recently. Running into the living room I grabbed the house phone and called 911 and told them that I had one man dying and one man dead to please hurry.

911 Dispatcher: 911 what's your emergency?
Me: Oh my God, two people are shot! I'm at 716 West Palm Lane! Please send someone ASAP! I think someone may be dead! Hurry!
911 Dispatcher: Ok Ma'am. Please stay on the line until the police and ambulance arrive. Do you know what happened?
Me: I don't know! I was in the bathroom and I heard a scuffle and gunshots! I didn't know what was happening! I was too scared to come out! When I did I found these two both with gunshot wounds!
911 Dispatcher: Ok ma'am, stay calm. I hear the sirens approaching. Are the police there yet?
Me: Yes, I see the lights in the window! Thank God!
911 Dispatcher: Ok you can hang up now the officers are on the scene.

Running to the door to let the officers in they arrived with guns drawn. Once I identified m self as the caller they lowered their weapons.

"Miss, are you hurt do you need help?" the first officer asked.

"No I'm not hurt, but there are two people shot inside. Hurry one might not make it!"

Sounds of radios and sirens filled the air on the quiet tree lined street. Police tape covered the whole front of the house as Jimmy was being lead away on a stretcher. All his neighbors lined the driveway trying to get a peek at what happened behind the walls of that house. The whispers of stories being told was hilarious.

"I heard he was a pimp."

"I heard he was a drug dealer."

"I heard he had a sex trafficking ring."

And so on the stories went making assumptions about what happened to cause him to be shot and another man to be murdered in house. The neighbors couldn't get enough of the drama and had always wondered how such a young man could afford such a nice house. Getting into a squad car to go down to the station to give a statement I was numb. It felt like a lifetime ago that I walked through that front door with a bottle of Hennessy in my hand. Never would I have imagined that it by the end of the night that someone would be going to the morgue and the other one going to the hospital clinging for his life.

Hours and hours at the station answering question after question, being drilled backwards and forward to get the facts straight had me exhausted. I was all cried out. I just wanted to go get my daughter, hug her and tell her how much I love her. Now I had to go through the trouble of telling not only my daughter, but Carlos's family what happened tonight.

Finally I was released and given back my property. Turning my phone on, I had a full mailbox of urgent messages and text. Nobody knew what was going on but Peyton. She was the only one I called so she must have told Carlos' and my mom what happened. Everybody else was just calling to be nosey and see what happened. I won't be calling them back, only the essentials first. My mind was still too numb to fully grasp the situation. Texting Peyton telling her I was on my way, I called my mom first to tell her I was fine. Then I called Carlos's mom and broke the news to me. She broke down saying that her baby couldn't be gone over something so senseless. I tried my best to console her but it was no good, she was a broken woman who just lost her eldest child only son. Sitting in my car in front of Line's house I looked down and realized my clothes are covered with blood. It was no way possible that I was going to let my little girl see me in this condition. It was bad enough that I already had to break the news that she would never see her dad ever again, let alone see her mother looking like I had committed the crime. Calling Peyton I asked her to bring me a wet wash cloth and a clean shirt to change into. Thinking back on the last 24 hours I was in shock, and as soon as Peyton seen the state I was in she just hugged me while we cried together. She never asked me exactly what happened or how, but somehow she knew that this was probably going to be a turning point in our lives. With her arm around my shoulder she ushered me inside. "Mina is still sleeping; you should go lie down in my room and get yourself together before you fall apart." Peyton said handing me a blanket. Moving on auto pilot, I peeled of my clothes and tried to sleep, but all I could see when I closed my eyes was the scuffle between Jimmy and Carlos, followed by the gunshots and all out pandemonium. Sitting up in the bed the sobs just wretched from the pit of my stomach making me gag. I caused this whole situation. Peyton ran in the room when she heard me wailing only to find me sitting in the middle of her bed, clutching the pillow as tears streamed down my face.

"Why?! Why did I agree to do it? Look what I did?!" I sobbed uncontrollably.

"My daughter is fatherless! I murdered my child's father!"

"Shhhhsh, clam down! You didn't do anything! Stop saying that! He was crazy and you can't control a person's emotions and reactions. Here take this Xanax so you can get some sleep. We'll talk some more when you get back up. We can get through this together sis; I promise I have your back." Peyton whispered as I closed my eyes. Haunting visions filled my mind as I attempted to fall asleep. I had seen things that would make a grown man have nightmares and now I didn't think I would ever be the same again.

• • • • • • • ● • • • • • • • • •

The next week went past in a flash and I was numb to the pain of it all. Jimmy had officially been arrested after the doctors gave him the medical clearance. The cops said that if he knew that this guy was going to try to rob him then he should have called the cops, not tried to handle it himself. They were also trying to figure out if I was at fault because I was the catalyst in this whole situation. So many what ifs ran through my brain. Like what if I just called the cops, or what if it had been Jimmy in the morgue instead of Los? What if I had never bumped into Jimmy at the coffee house? This whole situation could have turned out differently if he just made one phone call instead of getting his gun. I couldn't even look at him let alone speak with him. I never imagined that he would react that way and now my life is all in shambles because I dated him. Even though I had been questioned several times but there were no charges were being brought against me. I just so happened to be the cause and in the middle of the whole situation. The police did tell me that I would be needed again once Jimmy went on trial; I would have to testify if the evidence proved my story. I figured by the time that happened I would be in a better place mentally because right now I was just barely holding it together for Samya.

Trying to keep a brave face and still be a good mother was mentally exhausting. It would be all good until, I heard a song that reminded me of him. Or someone would say something that he always said, the tears would just well up in my eyes. You never realize how much a person is all around your life until they are gone. And I felt a hole in my chest that felt like it would never close. We had been staying at Peyton's because I didn't want the reminders of him surrounding me. Peyton did me the favor of getting his clothes together to be donated. She also became my middle person or moderator; any and all question went through her first. Peyton was more than my best friend; she was my sister and a second mom to Mina. I was so grateful to have her by my side even though I was a hot ass mess. Carlos was buried the following Wednesday after the whole ordeal. Peyton helped his mom with all the arrangements, down to what he should be buried in. It's funny how when your alive people act like they don't know you, but as soon as you die be the first one crying over your casket. The Catholic Church where is going home ceremony was packed with standing room only. And the wake that followed was something out of a movie. It was a parade of cars parked outside his mother's house and a huge cookout. I don't know who thought it appropriate to hire a DJ for a funeral, but his younger sister said we should be celebrating his life and crying over his death. I could understand the sentiment, but I just couldn't bring myself to enjoy the festivities around me. Peyton knew me better than anyone, probably even myself. That's why she took the weight off of me, because she knew that my mental state could break at any moment. Samya couldn't understand why she wouldn't be able to see her Papa again and why everyone was so sad. The only thing that kept me from losing my mind was the constant flow of Zanny's and Grey Goose floating thru my system.

CHAPTER 4
Short and Sweet

Days turned into weeks, weeks into months of just going thru the motions. I had become a shell of my former self. Samya was spending most of her time with Peyton because I just couldn't cope with her on a daily basis. It took everything in my being to get dressed and go to work daily and that was strictly out of necessity to pay my bills. Carlos' mother constantly called me to check on my and Samya but she mostly talked to Peyton since I was usually somewhere sleep or just in a daze. I started losing weight, my hair started falling out and I really didn't care about my appearance as long as what I had on was clean. I turned into a recluse who only wanted to drink and pop pills to keep the demons from haunting me when my eyes closed. I just wanted to not feel anything for a little while, or I just wanted to be live again versus the shell of the woman I used to be.

So one rare morning, after months of feeling like shit as soon as I opened my eyes, I woke up and my first thought wasn't about Carlos or Jimmy or guilt. I jumped up and felt the urge to get my life on track before it was too late. The first step towards getting back to the old me was cleaning up the pig stay for townhouse that I lived in. To say it was a mess was being nice, it was horrendous and now I understood why no one wanted to actually come inside. For the past couple of months I lived off of take out and food that other people had prepared for me. Mountains of take out containers and trash covered every surface in my kitchen. My laundry was scattered all over the place from me just grabbing whatever to have something to cover my body. Clean clothes mixed with dirty clothes mixed with out of season clothes covered every piece of furniture. Piles of unopened mail covered every surface waiting to open and paid. I had a lot to tackle and today was as good as any to do just that. And I missed my baby girl. Peyton had been great to me and her, taking on the role of unofficial mommy to my little girl while I sorted my life out. Today was the first morning I woke up and didn't immediately pop a pill and take a shot to get my day started; it was looking like a great day. If things kept up at this rate, everything would fall back into place sooner rather than later.

Calling Peyton, I told her my plans for the day and what I attempted to get done. She sounded surprised to hear me sound so clear and lucid after of months of me not being able to form a coherent sentence when we talked. Grabbing a shower and a cup of coffee I tackled the house first. Laundry, dusting, and mopping had me working up an appetite that had been replaced with a Grey Goose diet. Cleaning out the fridge proved that I had absolutely nothing to eat even if I was hungry. That was now number one on my list of things to do. I wanted to have baby girl for a little while. I needed to feel her tiny arms wrapped around my neck pouring unconditional love back into my heart. I knew I wasn't capable of taking on that responsibility of raising her myself again until I kicked my pill habit. It would impossible for me to function on the level needed to be alert enough to keep her out of trouble.

After I put the last load of clothes in the dryer I grabbed my keys, phone, purse, and grocery list off the counter. Looking around, I was surprised it only took up half of my day to get the house back to how it's supposed to look. Hopping in my ride I went to the store closest to my house so I could hurry back home and wait for Peyton to bring baby girl over. Even my car needed an over haul from the piles of old food and trash covering the seats. I couldn't believe how easily it was for me to block out all the necessary chores and fall into a depression so deep that I wanted to kill myself at times. My fear was leaving this life and leaving my daughter alone with no one to protect her. It was unfair and I refused to have my child growing up wondering whether her father and I loved her. She was the best thing that ever happened to both of us and she deserved to feel the love even if she only had one parent left. Before I knew I had zipped thru the whole store in no time. Checking over my list one more time before I leave the grocery store and I can feel someone's eyes on me staring from the produce section. Looking up my eyes had a long way to travel since he was so long. 6^3, brown skin, built like a line backer, eyes so chinky it looked like he was squinting and a smile that just lit up the room like he had a personal sun walking around with him. He disarmed me with the way he was staring me straight in my eyes. Once our eyes met it was pure poetry. Even with me looking like death warmed over I could see that he saw deeper than that, he saw my potential. Looking down I wanted to see what he saw when he looked at me. His piercing stare made me self conscience of my appearance, this raggedy ponytail, face scrubbed clean without an ounce of makeup, nails plain and unadorned with sweat pants had me feeling frumpy. I figured after taking stock of my appearance it was impossible that this fine ass dude was staring at me, he had to be looking at someone else. He just looked at me and smiled while waving a little to let me know he was definitely watching me. His smile was contagious because I smiled and waved back. He took that as an invitation and pushed his cart towards me, I noticed he had on a biker jacket carrying a helmet in his basket instead of groceries. He was a rider, a sexy rider at that. He piqued my interest which had not focused on another guy in a long while.

"Hi, I wasn't staring but I noticed that you had all healthy items in your cart. Can you help me pick out some fruit to make the perfect energy smoothie? I'm trying to get in shape." The handsome stranger asked.

"Looks can be deceiving, I buy what I like. Not what's healthy, but I'll try to help you. You don't look like you needed much help with getting in shape. You look pretty fit if I must say so myself." I said as I flirted with him. He had me smiling in less than five minutes of meeting; my cheeks flamed as we spoke and fondled fruit.

"Well thank you, I'm not really out of shape, just looking for a healthy alternative to fruit juice." He said watching my face as we talked.

"I can probably help you with that either way. What type of flavors are you into?"

"I like the tropical flavors."

"I would try strawberries, mango, pineapple and spinach. That gives you a good flavor and tons of energy." Leaning over I squeezed his forearm. It felt like a brick, all muscle. My face turned another shade of red as I realized I just touched him without asking and I liked it.

"Well I want to maintain what I have and decided that it was time to start making better food choices. By the way, my name is Blake. I've never seen you here before." He said as he extended his hand to shake mine.

"Kennedy, nice to meet you. Yeah I usually shop at night when it's quiet and I can take my time."

"It is all my pleasure! So what do you like to do in your free time Kennedy?"

"I like to read and hang out with my friends. I'm the mother of a smart precocious little girl. You know regular stuff."

"Have you ever been interested in riding on a crotch rocket at high speeds?"

"A what?"

"You know a crotch rocket, a bike, a motorcycle?"

"Oh, of course! I'm a little scared of getting hurt or killed." I said feigning concern, clutching at my chest.

"Well if you give me your number maybe I can take you for a ride. I promise to be safe and not get you killed." Blake said as he laid his hand over his heart.

"Sounds like a good offer, but right now I'm not in a place to have any sort of relationship with anyone. My life is a mess, but I could use a friend."

"Hey, it's no pressure in an actual date, just two adults going for a leisurely ride, enjoying the wind blowing thru our hair." He said

Biting lip I debated about how much I should tell him about my life at the moment. Today was the first day since everything happened that I wasn't on auto pilot. I figured it's been over six months since I even looked at a man like a man let alone been even remotely attracted to someone. And if I was honest with myself I missed being touched and held, I missed the companionship of being around a man. It couldn't hurt to have a male friend. It just so happened that he was sexy as shit.

"Sure, I'll give you my number. Call me and we will see about that ride. Ok?" I said.

"That's all I'm asking." He said as he pulled his cell out of his pocket to take my number.

"609-510-0010"

"Ok, I'll give you cal Kennedy. And Thanks for helping me with my smoothie recipe."

"No problem Blake. It was nice meeting you."

Rushing home, I smiled as I drove home. It's funny how a kind word or gesture can make you feel so good inside. And Blake had definitely made my day with his sweet words. As I put away my groceries and started a light dinner for myself, Peyton, and Samya, I couldn't wait to hear from him. Looking around, I decided to finish putting away the laundry that I washed when I hear a car door shut in front of my house. Racing down the steps I was excited to see my baby and bestie. Snatching the door open I see my daughter racing to the door with her arms extended waiting to jump in my arms. Lifting her off her feet, it felt good to have her in my arms again. The love coming off of her was so strong and pure I could have held onto her all day just like that. Kissing her and smelling her hair conjured up good memories of play dates and bubble baths. I missed my little muffin and I could tell that she was happy to be in my arms again.

"Mommy I missed you! I love Aunt Peyton but I want to come home with you!" Samya said in her high pitched 2 year old voice. Looking in her face her eyes were far wiser than her years on earth.

"You will Hunni, as soon as mommy feels better. I told you, I promise you can come home and sleep in your own bed. You can come over whenever you want to, your mom would be happy for the company I'm sure. Why don't you go up to your room and find some toys that you haven't played with in a while. We can take some of those back to my house when we leave. Is that ok?" Peyton asked Samya getting down on her haunches so they were eye to eye.

"Yes Auntie! I would like that! How long before Mommy gets better? Are you taking medicine mom?"

"Soon Hunni, soon. I promise!" I answered before Peyton could reply.

Grabbing her blanket she went upstairs to her room to see what else she could take to her aunt's that she hadn't brought her.

Peyton walked around my place and looked around. Surprised that after all these months that I actually cleaned my house and went grocery shopping. This was the first time she walked in that it wasn't dark as a cave and as smelly as a boy's locker room. I could tell that even though she was trying to keep it together for me, she had her own thing going on. I couldn't tell if it was something good or something dark. I hoped that she was happy. We hadn't really had a conversation about anything except what had to do with Samina. I missed how we used how we used to be with each other. As she sat at the island and grabbed a glass and poured some Grey goose over ice, I knew that today was as good as any to catch up on her life. I walked around the island and hugged her; we had been friends so long that I couldn't remember not being friends with her. And through this whole situation she showed me that she was a real friend and she had my back through everything. Even though I couldn't find the words to describe my gratitude, I hoped that she could feel the love pouring out of me.

"I felt like I hadn't had a real conversation with you in forever. What's up?" I asked taking the seat across from her pouring myself a drink.

"Nothing, I met a guy a couple of months ago. It's been so good so far that I don't want to jinx it! I'll introduce y'all soon; I just didn't know when would be a good time. I see you got this house together, I was giving you until next week and I was going to do it!"

"I had to! I woke up and was like my life is a mess! But back to you, I'm happy you found someone, you deserve to be happy. I can't wait to meet him."

"Bitch, thank goodness you came back to us! I didn't think that I would ever see any semblance of my best friend again. I thought we had lost you and I didn't know what would bring you back. That little girl is a spitfire and she keeps me on my toes. Her attitude is just like yours but she looks just like her father." Peyton said. As soon as the words left her mouth she regretted it.

"I'm sorry; I shouldn't have said anything about him. I'm sorry!"

Just like that my mood had shifted back onto things that I wanted to forget. Grabbing the bottle I took a swig straight from the bottle. Reaching into the cabinet I popped a pill. I was feeling good until she brought reality crashing back down on me with that one comment. Peyton watched me as I tilted my head back waiting for the lethal cocktail to take effect.

"I'm so sick of you self medicating! I need my friend back, Samya needs her mother! You keep trying to numb yourself but you'll never get over it if you never let yourself feel again. And it's not fair because you're not the only one hurting." She screamed at me with tears flowing down her face.

Looking at her my heart broke for what I was doing to the people who loved me. At the same time I was in my own living hell and was just trying to keep myself from drowning in despair. Grabbing her hands so would stand so I could hug I said,

"I'm sorry. I have been being selfish just thinking about me. I'm hurting inside Peyton, real bad. Every time I think about Carlos I feel like my chest is going to explode. I feel so guilty when I'm not on the pills. And every time I look at Samya all I see is her dad. I know I need help but right now I just don't want to feel anything. Because when I feel the pain is so great it feels like it is going to consume me." I said as the tears started flowing down my face. Sitting back down, we just looked at each other with tears silently running down both our faces. Grabbing her hands I didn't know what else to say, I wanted to be better but I just couldn't take the risk of closing my eyes and seeing that horrible scene playing behind my eyes all the time. Getting up I put the final touches on the food even though my mood was blown and I really didn't feel like eating now. But I acted like I did and I put on a brave front for Samya. Peyton was watching me like a hawk but didn't broach the subject again. She knew that the more she pushed the deeper I would go back into the place that I was clawing my way up from. Focusing my energy on the one good thing in my life, Samya, I tried to make this one of her best days ever. We talked and played. I painted her nails and let her do my makeup. I missed her little fingers and voice. I realized how much joy this girl brought to my life and I was thankful. I was really thankful to have a piece of her father still with me, thankful that I survived that night, and thankful to have a friend that loved me enough to love my daughter when I couldn't.

Lying on the couch with Samya between us Peyton decided that they would stay the night. She wanted me to have an opportunity to spend more time with Samya but she also wanted to keep an eye on me. So after putting Samya in her bed we headed to the back deck to have a couple more drinks and catch up with adult talk.

"First let me say Thank You. Thank you for everything Peyton. I just want to thank you for always having my back and thank you for loving my daughter like she's your own."

"Girl please, we've been best friends since we were 8 years old when your sister tried to pull my hair! I love you like a fat kid love cake! Now cut it with the sentimental bullshit. I want to tell you what's really going on with me!" she gushed.

"That's the face you make when it must be getting borderline serious with this guy!" I said.

She just covered her mouth and giggled. "Yup, and he is the shit! I think I'm in love! Oh shit! You ever hear those words come from out of my mouth before?! I got it bad!"

I just stared at her in awe. Peyton always dated but never took one dude serious enough to even consider saying "I Love You". She was always dating casually and never brought the guys around because Carlos would rag on them hard. He hated every guy she dated and told them that he thought they weren't good enough for his sister. Carlos and Peyton always had a close relationship and he took every opportunity to make she was ok; he loved her like he loved me. Looking around I squinted my eyes and whispered, "Where is my best friend and who is this imposter that looks and talks just like her?" we both just laughed and laughed until it hurt.

For the next 3 hours we talked about good times and food, laugh and drank until our stomachs and our faces hurt from laughing, and then dragged ourselves inside so we could crash on my sectional. I was feeling like my old self again. I felt happy and carefree. Closing my eyes I thought to myself that today was definitely a good day.

· · · · · · · · ● · · · · · · · · ·

The following week went past in a flash. Getting up going to work every day, followed by picking Samya up from the sitter, and to dinner with Peyton kept my mind occupied. After I found out she was seeing someone I thought it was best if I gave her sometime to herself. It was time to figure out if she wanted to pursue it more deeply. She deserved to be loved and I wanted her to be happy. I forgot that I had even met someone at the store earlier in the week, so I was pleasantly surprised when my phone rang with a number I didn't recognize. Balancing my soda and bag in one hand I answered the phone out of breath as I unlocked my door.

"Hi, may I speak with Kennedy please?" a deep sensual voice said over the phone. I pulled the phone away from my ear so that I could look at the number again.

"This is she. Who is this?" I stated trying to get straight to the point thinking it was a reported or bill collector.

"This is Blake. We met at the grocery store the other day. You helped me with a smoothie recipe. By the way it was great." He said smiling all in his voice.

"Oh hi, Blake! I'm surprised you called. I totally forgot that I gave you my number. So what's up with you?"

"I was wondering if you wanted to go to lunch and a ride one of these days. I'm available whenever you are."

Putting him on speaker, I pulled down my calendar to see what I had going on this week. I had already decided to take off Wednesday and Thursday because Peyton wanted to do some things for herself.

"Oh ok how about Thursday? I'm off work and could use something to pass the time besides sitting in the house all day. I do have to pick my daughter up around 4pm from school." I said

"Cool, well text me your address and I'll pick you up. Wear something that covers your skin and comfortable shoes. I'll see you Thursday at 11am?"

"How about we do it at 1pm and I'll meet at the same grocery store we met at. Is that ok?"

"Sure Kennedy, I look forward to spending some time with you. Enjoy the rest of your week. Until then Ciao!" he said before he hung up the phone.

Trying to gain my wits I was thinking about what the weekend had in store for me. He might have been interested in something more than a ride but that was all that was going to happen. After everything, I just didn't think that it would be wise to start seeing someone else. Grabbing a microwave dinner out of the freezer I decided to check the mailbox while it cooked. My neighbor was out there speed walking with her dog, we waved at each other. The people on this block had been weird ever since Carlos had passed. They watched and talked from the distance, never trying to figure out the whole story. I didn't let it bother me though, people will always have something to say about you and what you have going. Sorting through the mail it was nothing but bills, brochures and one letter that was addressed to me with no return address. Looking at the envelope, you could tell that someone had put some effort into it but I couldn't imagine what or who sent it. Taking off my shoes to rest my aching feet I slip my finger under the tab to open the letter. Immediately my heart starts racing as I see black dead rose petals fall to the floor. Opening the letter there was only one line scrawled across the paper:

Revenge is a dish best served cold

Dropping the letter to the floor I was worried and afraid as to why someone would send this to me! Jumping up from the couch I ran to the kitchen and grabbed my two best friends: Grey Goose and Xanax. Popping two followed by a shot of Goose I just wanted it to all go away. I couldn't even make myself go back and pick the envelope up to inspect it again. It gave off a negative aura and I didn't want that energy rubbing off on me. Running the water in the shower I stepped under the hot spray and let the pills work their magic. The water hid the fact that I was crying my eyes out. Every time that I believe that I am finding my footing and things are getting better, but in reality they are only getting worse. Reaching to the bottle that I left on the sink I grab the Goose and take another swig. Clutching the bottle to my chest I just sat in the tub letting the water wash away all my frustrations. Who would send me a letter talking about revenge when I didn't do anything to anyone? I just lost my daughter's father and now I have someone threatening me? Life was beginning to become too much. Taking another sip I just sat there in a daze. Once the water turned cold and I started shivering I dragged my ass out the shower and wrapped myself in a towel. I was so exhausted I didn't dry my hair or get dressed just hopped under the blankets wet and allowed the Zanny and Goose to take me away. The goal was to go to a peaceful place where not even my worse thoughts couldn't penetrate.

It was short lived that the night would be a peaceful one, my mind was not at rest giving me nightmares. That night dreams of monsters and demons with pointy teeth and red eyes invaded my sleep. Weird people grabbing at my ripping my skin until rivers off blood surrounded me, drowning me. Then there were the voices that kept chanting "Revenge is a dish best served cold!" Waking in panic as sweat poured down my back, it took me a minute to realize that it was only a dream, but the reality of my life came crashing back down on me. Sleep couldn't even give me peace because my subconscious wouldn't allow me to forget. Grabbing the pill bottle was my only solace. 2 more and finish off the bottle to get me through the night. Looking at the clock it was only 3:30am, meaning I had a lot of hours in the dark with nothing to keep me occupied but my thoughts. Something had to give or I was going to go crazier than I already was. The only thought that kept popping into my head was I just wanted it all to be over.

• • • • • • • ● • • • • • • • •

Sunlight peeking through my blinds encouraged me to get up. Things needed to be done, money needed to be made. The sun made the headache that was trying to take root behind my eyes seem like a train was barreling through my head. I had to get up and take something or else I would be stuck in the bed all day. Throwing my legs over the side of the bed, stepping over wet clothes and towels I almost didn't remember what happened last night until I seen the letter on the floor. Memories of last night flooded me making me sick to stomach. Running to the bathroom I made love to the porcelain god. The more I tried to calm down, the more I stared to freak out. Dry heaving with nothing in my stomach made me weak. After what felt like hours I checked my appearance and was sad at the reflection staring back at me in the mirror. Dark circles under my eyes, blotched red skin surrounded my mouth; my complexion was dull, hair limp. I looked how I felt and

I had no idea how to get back to me. One bad careless decision was ruining my life. I wanted to be better for my daughter and I wanted a good quality of life back. Debating on going into work or calling out, I had been taking more and more days off from work. My money was funny and that made me decide that being out the house was better than being here with idle time to think. Grabbing a quick shower and throwing my hair in a ponytail I headed into work.

Everyone in the office knew what happened with me since the newspaper decided to publish the story, since a murder/love triangle was news. Nobody said anything about it, but I could tell that I was the topic of discussion when I wasn't in the office. I was just here for a paycheck either way and could care less what they thought. I took lunch at my desk to avoid the office gossip; my life was way more real than any of these bitter ass old women I worked with. The menial work task kept me focused on something other than myself and my problems for a while. All I wanted to do was get off work get another bottle and some more pills. Being fucked up kept me from fucking up.

Calling Peyton to check on Samya she said everything was good. Peyton seemed to be in good spirits, I'm pretty sure it had something to do with her mystery lover. Mina always knew how to brighten my day even if she was only a toddler. It felt good to talk to baby girl but I was still in a bad place mentally. I wanted to die, but knew that Samya would be a parentless child. No child asks for that, to be in this world without anyone that truly cared about them. Rushing in my house to crack the bottle and get my dosage, I wanted to escape reality for a little while. Lying on the couch with my head laid back I waited for the drugs to take effect, sleep was what I was after. As soon as I dozed off my phone rang. Waking up out of a drug induced sleep made me loopy. Reaching for the phone I never checked the caller ID.

"Hello? Hello?"

Nothing.

Hanging up and I check the caller ID, it was a blocked number. Laying back down dismissing the call as a wrong number I tried to grasp that little bit of sleep that I was clinging to. Not even 5 minutes passed before the phone rang again with the same bull shit. Same thing, just breathing in my ear followed by a high pitched female voice:

Revenge is dish best served cold!

Maniacal laughter that was so Erie I almost thought I imagined it. The sound completely waking out my sleep and making me drop the phone. Jumping up I turned on all the lights and checked all the windows. Who wanted revenge and why were they invading my space? Calling my house and sending me threatening letters? I had never had any problems with anyone, and no one knew the real story about what happened at Jimmy's house except Peyton. And she was my best friend, one of the only people I could trust without a doubt, I knew she wouldn't call me or send anything to my house knowing how fragile my state of mind was. For goodness sake she had my daughter and loved her like her own. Taking 2 more pills because that phone call blew my shit, I knew it would be a couple of hours before I would fall back to sleep. Sitting in my living room with every light on in the house I was scared and alone. This whole situation had me on edge; I was nervous with worrying and couldn't rest until I knew my family was ok. My heart couldn't take it to lose someone else so soon. I texted Peyton to make sure that the threat hadn't reached my daughter. It was crazy and I had no idea who was antagonizing me, I worried about her a Samina being there by their selves. Panicking, because she wouldn't respond or answer the phone, I threw on some shoes and hopped in my car. Please God let them be safe and ok because I would die if something happened to them because of my selfish actions. Racing through the streets of Pleasantville my mind was focused on one thing, laying eyes on the people I loved more than I loved myself. That would be the only solace that I had tonight if everything was ok.

Coming to an abrupt halt in front of Peyton's house I raced towards the door with my set of keys in my hand. It was already after 11 pm, all the lights were off except for a soft glow in the living room. Heart beating erratically while I fumbled with the keys, I cursed under my breath. Forcing the key in the lock, what I seen I had never expected. There were candles lit everywhere, the scent of vanilla and honey thick in the air. Rose petals covered every surface, with R Kelly singing "Give me some of your 12 play"; I heard giggles followed by splashing. Stopping dead in my tracks I noticed a helmet next to the steps.

"Peyton! It's me! I was calling and texting you! Is everything ok?" I yelled from the bottom of the steps. The compulsion to run up the steps was great, but the ambiance of the house kept my feet rooted in place. If she had company I didn't want to impose or see them in a compromising position, outing images in my head that I would never be unseen. Water sloshed again, I could hear the drops as she walked across the floor. The deep male voice sounded familiar but I couldn't place from where followed by heavy footsteps, you tell he was moving around, "Who is that? And why do they have keys to your house?" the man said. "That's my bestie, and her daughter is here so of course she has keys!" I hear Peyton whisper.

"I'm coming down, let me put something on. Give me couple of minutes." Peyton yelled down.

Going in the kitchen I turn on faucet to rinse a cup to get a drink out of the refrigerator. Closing the door I see pictures that Samya made. The imagination of a child can take you places that an adult mind could ever fathom, that's why seeing picture depicting her, her father, and me created a tug at my heart. Pictures of her with her father, her and Peyton all with smiling faces broke my heart. With tears streaming down my face, I quickly wiped them away. I was sick of being sad every time someone mentioned Los or Samya said something about her father. I knew that eventually I would get to that place of peace; it was just taking too long. Drinking the rest of the water, I started rummaging around looking for something stronger than could take the edge off. Leaning down in the fridge I found a half bottle of wine, but as soon as I got ready to stand up, I could feel another presence in the room with me. The presence was so magnetic that my eyes automatically scanned from the soles of his feet to the thickness of his calves. His skin was smooth and oiled, I was afraid if I looked higher for fear of what I would see. I adverted my eyes and finished looking in the fridge. I heard another lighter set of footsteps coming towards me.

"Is everything ok?" Peyton asked breathless.

"I'm just grabbing some wine, I needed something stronger than water to keep me sane. You want some, grab the glasses." I said with my head in the fridge. Turning I was face to face with Blake from the grocery store. I damned near walked into his perfectly sculpted torso. Throwing his t shirt on, I just stood there with my mouth hanging open. I had no idea what to say or if I should just act like we never met. Looking at his body, I could feel a longing in being that made me want to drool. He looked better out of his clothes than in.

"I seen you called, I was a little busy though. Sorry I didn't answer. You finally get to meet my friend. Blake, meet my sister/best friend Kennedy. This is Samina's mom." She said gesturing between us.

"It's nice to finally meet the guy who put a smile on my best friends face. I have heard nothing but good things about you." I said extending my hand to his.

She looked smitten making me hold my tongue and not speak a word of meeting him earlier in the week. It made sense that he would want to meet during the day, Peyton was at work during that time.

"Let me go check on Samina real quick, the talking might have woke her. Kennedy, pour me glass too." Peyton said dashing back up the steps. Blake turned and looked at me with pleading eyes.

"Aye, I didn't know you and Peyton were friends. Please don't tell her that you know me. I really like her and I want to see where this is going. You looked like you needed a friend. Please, I beg you?!" he whispered.

"No problem, I won't say a word. But you owe me." I whispered back.

Peyton came walking in with a flourish, sweat pants, tank top, and bare feet hair pulled up in a ponytail. Even though I could tell she was upset she would never say it. She was my friend, thru thick and thin, good and bad times. She knew I was hurting and decided to act like I didn't interrupt her getting ready to get her back blown out. I felt like shit bussing up her groove but the angst was too much for me to ignore. I had to see her to make sure that everything was ok. She could be mad right now, but it would be short lived. I wouldn't get comfortable, I just needed to see now I could go back to my own house and try to chase away the boogie man.

I looked at the clock mounted over her stove and seen how late it was. Standing, I started gathering my keys and phone, when Blake walked back in fully dressed.

"Well Baby, let me let you handle your business with your girl. Call me, we'll do something this weekend." Blake said as he leaned down and kissed her. Grabbing her booty, he grabbed his keys and helmet off the counter. Winking at me he left I had this feeling in the pit of my stomach that this wouldn't be the last time I seen him. Sitting at the island with a glass of wine in my hand I felt something that I never thought I would feel, Jealousy. I was hating so bad at that moment that Peyton's life was so easy. It's like everything that I wanted, Peyton had it. Nice little condo, career that she loved, and the guy that I thought could possible keep my mind off of what was going on in my mind. I wanted her life, or at least I thought I did. In my twisted little warped world my life was falling apart at the seams and I had no idea how to get it back together. Trying to hide the larceny in my heart, I smiled at her.

"So I rushed over here because I keep getting these letters with the words "Revenge is a dish best served cold!". Well it's only been 2 letters but the first one had dead roses in the envelope. I was calling and calling and calling. And you weren't responding so I assumed that something was wrong. I rushed right over to check on you and Samya. I never expected you to have company. I apologize for messing up your groove." I said as I stood to hug her.

"Girl, it has always been chicks before dicks! We've been friends, more like sisters since before we even liked boys. It will always be another opportunity to fuck him. He likes me and understands our situation a little. Oh well, he'll get over it and if not oh well. Why don't you stay here tonight? You can sleep in the bed with Samya and take her to school. I'm pretty sure she would really like that." Peyton said as she moved around downstairs blowing out candles.

"I think I will. It's already 4 am and I'm too hyped up to actually sleep." Gulping down the last drop of wine, I walked upstairs and snuggled under the covers with my baby. Hearing her even breathing and rapid heat beat lulled me into a restless sleep. No dreams came that night, but the jealousy was slowly turning into a monster churning below the surface waiting to attack.

• • • • • • • ● • • • • • • • •

Lying on the couch watching reruns of Nip/Tuck on cable I was already zoning off the Grey Goose and Xanax I had taken as soon as I stepped into the door from work. I called it the 2 for two. 2 shots and two pills put me at ease and allowed me to make it through the day. Hearing the alert for a missed text message on my phone I finally gathered up enough energy to get up and check it.

Blake: Hey it's Blake.

Me: Hey I didn't expect to hear from you.

Blake: Yeah well I figured after the other night I
shouldn't text but then I remember a conversation
that Peyton and I had about her best friend.

Me: And why would I be the topic of discussion?

Blake: I was just wondering what happened to her friend
that she would have to leave her only child with someone
else. And I really liked you when I met you.

Me: And? You do know the girl you were
laid up with is my best friend?

Blake: That something traumatic had happened and now that she was
worried that you might have a self medicating problem. I know that
y'all all really good friends. I'm not trying to come in between that.

Me: Well how about I'm grown, and I got everything under
control. Is there another reason why you text me?

Blake: Chill! I wasn't saying it like that. I'm saying
I like to party a little myself. If you're down, I have
something you might want to really try……..

Instead of me ending the conversation right then, my curiosity got
the best of me, kept me asking questions.

Me: What would that be?

Blake: X

Me: I never tried and always wanted to. If you want to go there,
you're more than welcome to come over. I'm not doing ish
you can come over. I heard you can be on a trip for hours.

Blake: Yeah, it takes a while for you to come down. But I'll be
with you the whole time, no worries. Text me you're addy

Me: 564 Marien Ave. Park in the driveway

Blake: Be there in a half

Closing the conversation I took stock of what I was about to do and
what my house looked like. Morally I was at an impasse, I was about

to do something that I shouldn't and I didn't really care about the consequences that would follow. Physically everything seemed to be in place since I spent most of my time lying around in the bed. Hopping in the shower I wanted to shake off some of the effects of the drugs and liquor I already consumed so I could be on point when this guy showed up. After washing and shaving quickly, I threw on some shorts, tee, with long socks on my feet and my hair piled in a messy bun completed the look. Walking back to living room I put on a movie that I wanted to see for a while and got comfortable waiting for Blake to show up. I know I should have had reservations about inviting him over but I didn't. I was not only attracted to him and the thrill of doing something taboo; I couldn't wait to be in the presence of a man. I couldn't resist. This road of self destruction gave me heady rush that couldn't compare to any feeling that I felt at the moment because I felt like shit most of the time. This was a change of pace; my heart was racing in anticipation.

In the mean time I called Peyton. Partly to check on my baby and mostly to see what she was up to. I would hate for her to pop up and catch Blake here, it wasn't anything going on with us, yet. After talking to Samya about our weekly plans, I bussed it up with my girl for a while. All was good on her front and she was rushing me off the phone talking about getting ready for bed. We blew kisses over the phone and promised to have dinner tomorrow at my place. Just as we hung up the phone I could hear the motorcycle approaching my property. Looking out the blinds I saw him saunter up the driveway with the swag of hustler. Helmet in his hand while his long legs were covered in black jeans with Timbs topped with a white tee under a leather jacket. Opening the door he smelled manly, like Sandalwood and Patchouli. Leaning in to hug me I could feel his corded muscles wrapping around my torso. Everything about him was appealing to me at this point, I was turned on already and we hadn't even spoken a word to each other yet.

Stepping back to let him in the door, "Hey Blake, thanks for coming over. Come have a seat. You want something to drink?" I asked.

"Yeah just some water, and bring yourself some. I hope you don't mind I brought a movie for us to watch. You got some snacks? I wanted to take you for a ride, but I don't know how good of an idea that is." he said.

"I haven't really been in the mood to do much lately; we can go for a ride some other time. Maybe, who knows?"

Going in the kitchen I grabbed some tortilla chips, salsa, sliced fruit, and two bottles of water. Putting everything on a tray, I walked back into the living room to find Blake with his shoes and shirt off with a table full of paraphernalia. He was breaking down the Dutch to roll the weed up in. I hadn't smoked in years but I could tell by the smell that it was some good weed. Next to that he had a baggy of powder and a couple of pills lay out on the table. Sitting the tray down I just gazed wondering what I had gotten myself into. He said party, I had no idea he meant a real live party, I had only dabbled never went full Monty.

Rolling up a $5 dollar bill, he leaned over and took a hit of coke. Holding out the rolled up bill he handed it to me. "You want a hit? It will help you relax a little. You seem tense." He said.

"I'd rather not, I never dabbled. I would rather just try the X."

"Well this helps boost what your high, the weed helps mellow it out."

I was feeling the pressure to try everything, but wasn't ready to go that far. It seemed like he was going on 100 while I was still just warming up.

"Well let me do the X first, I'll see if I want to try the coke too.

Handing me a pill I popped it back and chased it with some water. Putting the DVD in of Martin Lawrence Blue Streak I waited for the drugs to take effect. Lighting the blunt that he rolled I felt lose and limber. I was sitting there thinking, I must be immune because nothing was happening. And just as that thought crossed my brain as the blunt was almost gone, I felt the effects of the X. Tingly sensations on ever nerve ending had me squirming in my seat. It felt like I could feel every follicle of hair on my body like a massage. Running his hands up and down my arm felt like he was rubbing the sweet spot between my legs. Knees clenched tight against the pulsing of my clit had me panting. Kissing my shoulders as Martin found himself stuck in the shaft, I trembled every time I felt his breathe on my skin. I was more horny than I ever been in my whole life. He must have known that the first time would be like this because he just waited for me to get high enough.

Turning to look at him, he shook his head and with a smile leaned over and kissed my lips. I swear the sensations were so exaggerated it felt like every inch of my body was linked directly back to my coochie. His lips tugged at mine while coaxing me into opening wider to accept what he was offering. I moaned into his mouth as he put his hand up my shirt. The feel good feelings rushing through my body made me tremble with anticipation. I didn't know what he was going to do to me but wished he would hurry up and do it. I was so turned on that my hands moved on their own accord to touch myself. Slow sensual circles over my bud and I shuddered. I wanted him or anyone at that moment to fuck me until I was numb. I felt wanton with need and was ready to act on it.

Turning to Blake I said," You know us being here is wrong. But I liked you from the moment we laid eyes on each other. Even though Peyton is my best friend, I still want to fuck the shit out of you. I won't tell if you won't." Leaning over to lick his earlobe his whole body shuddered in response. "I would never try to come between you two, but I can't front. I wanted to fuck you right in the middle of the produce section when we met. Let me take your mind off of things for a while. Let me make you feel special like the queen you are." He said as he leaned over a teased my pebbled nipple through my shirt leaving a wet spot. I moaned and lay back on the couch with my legs cocked open. I wanted him to touch me where I had been touching myself but he had his own plans for my body. Running his hands up my spread legs he put gentle kiss on my inner thighs on his way up. A symphony of sounds escaped from my body combined with panting, squirming and moaning was all that I could do. The rush of doing something so taboo with my best friends guy, the drugs, and the fact that I hadn't been touched since before Los got murdered I came right on the spot. The sensation hit me waves, slow at first building into something fast and furious like a raging storm. Pulling my shorts down he revealed my naked lips with the pungent smell of arousal permeated the room. Looking up from between my legs like it was a buffet he seen after being starved and I was on the menu. He tasted me like it was the sweetest thing he ever tasted. He was shy about it or afraid, he was head first licking and nibbling on my lady parts until I came again. When I thought he had his fill he added a finger, and I came again with a scream. He made me cum 3 times without penetrating me, and he made me want him more than I wanted anyone in my life. I was almost incoherent

"Fuck me, fuck me, please just fuck me Blake!" I screamed out of breathe. I felt insatiable. In my mind it felt like I would always be horny as I was at that moment and that I could be fucked hard and still want more. Blake just stroked my skin, making it hot wherever he touched. My body was so sensitive; I was dying a slow death from pleasure overload. Standing up, shedding his pants he revealed what had been hidden from me. With no barriers obstructing my view, his dick was on front street and he was beautiful. His smooth complexion melted perfectly into this thick, chocolate, thick mushroom head, with veins that bulged making it look sinister. Just looking at him made my mouth water with anticipation of feeling him on my tongue. Kneeling at his feet I looked up at him from under my lashes. "Do you want me to suck your dick Blake? Because it looks like he wants to be sucked on." I said just a hairs breath away from the head. Straining while staring in my eyes through gritted teeth, "Kennedy, don't fucking play! Suck that shit like you trying to win an award!" Fisting his hand in my hair he looked me in my eye and said "Don't play when I'm on Kennedy. It's dangerous, and I want that pussy!" Grabbing him at the base of his cock, stroking him towards the tip, he grows bigger in my hand. Time was not of the essence since we had all night; I licked him like an ice cream cone on a cold day. Those long leisurely strokes of my tongue from the balls to the tip made him whimper. I worshipped that dick, taking it into my throat until I gagged then massaging his balls. I attempted to swallow him whole but was impossibly large. Over and over I took him into me, my wet soft mouth covering his hardness. I don't know how long I stayed like that but the more he moaned the wetter I got. In a tandem he had me obsessed with pleasing him. One hand on his balls the other circling my engorged clit and I could feel the climax coming on strong. Panting all erratic I felt the edges lapping over trying to be released when he stopped me. "Your pleasure is mine tonight. You are not allowed to get yourself off, that's my job. I want you to cum when I tell you!" Yanking me up by my ponytail he kisses so deeply I start to feel cum trickling down my inner thigh. The wetness made goose bumps raised on my body from being exposed to the air. I shivered from the breeze and anticipation. Bending me over the couch he entered me from behind slowly so that I could feel every inch as he penetrated for the first time. His initial thrust sent me into a series of orgasm that was never ending and plentiful. My body was wracked with a thousand little deaths with every stroke. I couldn't tell where one began and the other ended. The whole inside of my body clenched with each thrust making me feel like I had shattered into a 1,000 pieces and the only thing that was holding me together was him having me pinned to the couch.

We fucked on every surface. He fucked me hard at times making me beg for mercy, then slow and tender making love to body. He fucked me rough, pulling my hair choking me. He fucked me soft planting tender kisses all over my engorged skin. Doing a line of Coke between sessions kept the feelings high and kept us connected in a way that I had never been with anyone else. I was so aroused yet sore at the same time, but not sore enough to stop him. He took me every way possible and made me cry from doing things to my body that I had never experienced before. I had never been more thoroughly fucked in my entire life. Lying on the floor of the living room, legs intertwined, skin damp with sweat, with sunlight creeping around the edges, my mind couldn't even form a coherent thought from the pleasure overload. I wished at that moment that every night could be like this, filled with so much passion and mind blowing sex that some was never enough. No words were needed; we just laid in each other's presence until the silence turned into deep breathing. We both had work in a couple of hours and wanted to at least try to close my eyes before, either way sleep was calling us just as clock hit 7am. In that lucid state between sleep and dream when you're not sure what you see or hear, I imagined Peyton walking in on us tangled on my living floor. It had to be a dream because I wasn't beat out off my sleep. Blinking trying to clear my thoughts, I imagined I seen her disappointed face looking at the scene that stumbled on. Instead she turned on her heels and shut the front door quietly behind her as if she was never here.

Laying face down, naked I remember Blake telling me he was leaving. Grabbing the extra blanket that I left on the couch, he wrapped me up making me want to sleep deeper. Telling him to lock the door when he left, I felt him kiss my shoulder and telling me he would call later. Grabbing the pillow off the floor, I snuggled under the blanket and fell back to sleep.

• • • • • • • ● • • • • • • • •

Exhausted.

That was the only way to describe how I felt. It was no way that I was going to be even relatively No work, no play, just the bed the whole next day. I called my boss and told her that I had some family issues to take care of and would be there tomorrow bright eyed and bushy tailed. It took my body that long to recover from the drugs and beating that Blake put on me. The drugs had me out of my mind while he hurt me so bad that it felt good. The achy soreness between my legs proved that last night really happened. Everything seemed a little hazy and fuzzy around the edges making it hard to tell fact from fiction. I guess the combo of Xanax, X, Coke, and Grey Goose got me lose enough that I willing to do anything. Lying under the covers with the blinds shut and the lights off, I was thirsty, hungry, and sweaty. The come down was real and the effects were crazy on my body. I needed food and a shower but I still felt out of it. My motivation was in the gutter, so I just took some time to reflect on the events that had transpired. Dragging myself to the shower I just let the water beat down on me. The steam seemed to clear my mind and bring some clarity to my current situation. How did I really feel about last night? I loved every minute of it! I had never felt so free in my life. No worries or fears invaded my mind when I was up, only pleasant thoughts and feelings. On the flip side, I thought I would feel some type of way about fucking Blake knowing that he was Peyton's new thang. To be honest I didn't care, no I take that back. I didn't care who he was as long as the pleasure was so intense. I was concerned about how Peyton might feel if she found out, but I knew through thick and thin she had my back. She would never let something as small as a dude could never ruin our friendship that we had been building our whole lives. Stepping out the shower I hear the shrill of my cell ringing. Grabbing a towel running into my bedroom I tried to answer before the person hung up.

"Hello?"

"Well hello to you too! Are you ok? I've been calling you for hours with no answer. I called your job your boss said you called out to handle family business is everything ok? I wanted to know if you wanted to go with me to get your daughter an outfit for her school pictures."

"Oh hey girl, yeah I was feeling under the weather decided to stay home. You know sinus problems and all. When is Samina's pictures and why didn't you tell me? She is MY daughter you know!" I said getting upset that she was acting like Samya was her child. The drugs had me feeling short.

"1st of all, what the hell crawled up your ass today? 2nd I told you the other day that she had pictures coming up. And if you were a little more actively involved in your daughter's life, you would be calling me to go to the mall with you. Not the other way around. Obviously something is wrong on your end; call me when you're ready to have a real conversation without snapping on me! And check your raggedy ass attitude like you got a problem with me. You know Kennedy; I have the problem with you with your shady ass moves." Peyton said hanging the phone up in my ear. I was stunned, we had never had an argument let alone her get pissed enough at me to hang up in my ear. Our relationship was changing right before my eyes and I didn't know if it was because of me or we were just having growing pains.

Sitting on the side of the bed wrapped in a towel, while I rubbed fragrant coconut oil into my skin, the laughter just bubbled up from out of nowhere. Right, I thought. Whatever! It's funny that she's calling me acting like she's my child's mother. Acting like I should consult her about the affairs of my child! People help you out and then they believe that they are an expert on things that you've been doing forever. But it wasn't just this situation that had the undertones of something being wrong between us; it has been plenty of little signs that something was amiss with our relationship. I understood that she was hurt just as much as I was by Los' murder and I thought we bonded over it. Now I can see that it was much deeper than just pain, it was something else that I couldn't put my finger on. My appreciation and love for her was so deep I couldn't understand why she as lashing out at me. Some changes needed to made, and the first thing was getting my daughter back and stop depending on her so much emotionally. I loved her, but I loved me more. And it was no way that I would let her control what I did with my daughter. If I had to cut ties with her, it would hurt, but I'm built Ford tough, I would survive.

CHAPTER 5
Coming Down

"Can I speak to Kennedy please?" the professional voice on the other end of the phone stated.

Turning over to look at the clock I see that it read 11:47am. I was supposed to be at work at 9am and was still in the bed. Sitting straight up I cleared my throat before I spoke.

"This is she."

"This is Nancy from HR. I am calling you to inform you that you are no longer needed for the position that you hold. You have been taking off too many days with explanation or proof of the "family issues" you claim of why you are off. I'm sorry that I am calling you at home, but your boss said that you did a no call/no show today. Please drop your sledge and you're your work computer at the HR office. Your check will be ready. I hope that everything works out for you." she stated before hanging up the phone.

I yawned and stretched while trying to gather my thoughts about me. It had been 3 months since I had been seeing Blake. In those 3 months we had party and fucked in more ways than I can count. All those late nights lead to early mornings and me calling out because it was impossible for me to function enough to work. I thought that I still had control over the way my life was going, but now I could see that this crazy lifestyle that I was living was catching up to me. I wasn't worried about losing the job, I hated it anyway. The job was just a means to be able to provide for my child, I could find work somewhere else. It was no point in crying over things that I couldn't control.

I decided since I didn't have a job to go to anymore I might as well take it easy. Reaching into my night stand drawer I pulled out the little baggy of white powder. Putting a bump between my thumb and forefinger I inhale the potent potion. Letting my head fall back the affect was immediate. Opening my eyes I felt like I was floating and today wasn't so bad even though I had been fired. Walking into the bathroom I caught a glance of myself in the mirror. The concern over how I looked or what people thought of me had changed. I wasn't into impressing people if it wasn't absolutely necessary anymore. That thought process was showing now.

My eyes were puffy and glassy. Dark circles under my eyes and blotchy red skin made me look 10 years older than I was. My hair hung limp and brittle like a dirty doll baby. Turning the water on super hot I figured the heat could cleanse my mind, heart and body. Standing under the spray until it turned cold, I wrapped my body in towel. Looking through the closet I found a long Maxi dress that always looked good without much effort. Throwing it on it hung loosely like I borrowed it from someone 3 sizes bigger than me, but who really cared. Throwing on some gladiator sandals, lip gloss, tinted moisturizer, and wrapping my wet hair in a bun, I was ready to get this shit over wit.

Grabbing my keys, I stepped out on my doorstep only to step on an envelope. Leaning down I grabbed the unmarked envelope. Turning it over in my hands I started to get nervous. I knew what to expect before I even opened the letter. Looking around I didn't see anyone or anything that looked out of place. Not a single car or person was different than normal. Sliding my key under the flap I could see the rose petals before I took the note out. With tremble hands I read the words that were written:

Revenge, when oh when? Sooner or Later?

Throwing my door back open my heart was pounding in my chest. The drugs made me forget about these letters with the threats. Throwing all the contents of my purse right there in the foyer, I found the little pill that could make me forget. Running to the kitchen, I put my mouth under the running faucet and took the pill. Sliding down to the floor, I was shaken to my core. Who? Why? Deciding that being in this house only made things worse, I grabbed my stuff and got into the car. Speeding away from the curb, I must have looked like a mad woman running from something. Driving into the city, I was constantly looking in my mirrors to see if someone was following me. Between the Coke and the letters I was paranoid. So busy checking the mirrors that I almost crashed into the back of a car waiting for the traffic to move. Glancing around, I got that itch up my neck like someone was watching with malice intent. When you're running from demons that you can't see, everyone is a suspect.

As soon as the light turned green, I switched lanes and sped through the rest of traffic keeping a close eye on the cars in my peripheral. Pulling up to my now former job, I felt a trickle of sweat roll down my back. Parking in the space closest to the door a see a black Suburban, all tinted out creep past my car. The person never stopped and the person never revealed themselves. That could be the person or it couldn't. I had no basis to form a coherent thought on the why I was being harassed. Palms sweaty, I could barely open the car handle. Walking in past the receptionist, I never spoke or I never lifted my shades. For what? These people had been whispering and insinuating behind my back for months. No hard feelings, no feelings at all, just happy to be free from the demon of the corporate world. Getting off on the second floor, I walked through the doors labeled "Human Resources". Stopping at the receptionist desk to give her my name she sent me into the back office. I just wanted to get this over with so I could get on with my life. Signing the work release form I grabbed my check and headed to the bank. I wanted to do something nice for myself today. I deserved it after all the crap that I had been dealing with. Plus who knew when would be the next time I could treat myself since money wasn't going to be steady until I found another job.

Sitting in the car in front of the bank, I did another hit of Coke. It seemed like I needed the nose candy just to be semi functional. I wasn't an addict. But it did take the edge off and give me the confidence that I lost after Carlos's murder. Checking my nose in the mirror, I needed to make sure that I looked half decent before I ran into anyone else. Grabbing my purse to make the deposit, I hit the locks on the door before walking across the parking lot. Just as I walking in the bank two very familiar faces were walking towards. It was like God knew that I needed to be around people and never thought that he would put these two in my path. It was my little sister Tasha aka TaTa and her best friend Shiana. I hadn't seen TaTa since Los' funeral, and even then it barely registered she was there. I was that out of my mind with grief. Last time I stopped past my mother's house, she said that they were in Vegas "working". I didn't have any idea what working consisted of but judging by their jewels and designer clothes it must have been lucrative.

"TaTa and Shania is that y'all?!" I squealed looking over the top of my glasses. Both of them stopped in their tracks and looked at me. It was like to brick walls crashing into each other. Hugs, squeals, and un-understandable words were being exchanged between the three of us. We forgot where we were until the security guard walked over to us and asked us to keep it down.

"I don't have to keep shit down. I have a fat ass account with this bank. So either you want to keep my business or you going to let me hug my sister that I haven't seen in almost a years." my baby sister TaTa said. All while twisting her neck and rolling her eyes, I forgot how angry she can get if she is interrupted.

"Bitch, I just asked Mommy where you and my niece were. We been in town for a couple of weeks and wanted to hang out with y'all." TaTa said.

"Ooop, mom never told me. But I haven't seen or talked to mom in a couple of months. It's been a lot going on and Samya has been staying with Peyton. But yeah, y'all! Stop past later, I'll be home bored and could use the company." I said. Texting my number and address to the number that TaTa had rattled off. It was sad that I didn't realize that I hadn't spoken to my sister in a while or that I didn't have a working number to call her in an emergency situation. Some things needed to change with our relationship, she was my family. Turning to hug them both, they smelled as expensive as they looked. Watching them sashay out of the bank, men broke their necks to get a look while the women lusted after their physic and obvious wealth. I see them both take out their designer shades to cover their eyes from the blinding afternoon sun. Walking over to the latest Benz sitting on 20 inch rims, I see them hop in and pull off. I was impressed with whatever they had going on. They looked like money. I couldn't wait until later so I could find out what's up. Maybe whatever they had going on I could be a part of.

Rushing out the bank, my phone was going off. Looking down I had two separate messages, 1 from Peyton and 1 from Blake. Deciding that the less of two evils was Blake I opened his 1st.

> Blake: Hey Kennedy, what you doing later? I wanted to bring my friend over so he could party with us.
> Me: Ok, that's cool. The more the merrier. I'll see you later. Make sure you bring enough for all of us.
> Blake: Ok, see you then

Since I was already excited about seeing Blake I figured it was nothing that Peyton could say that would or could piss me off.

Peyton: Are you free? I need to speak with you in person?
Me: Yes, I guess I could come over now. Are you home?
Peyton: Yes
Me: I'm on my way

Sitting in my car I couldn't remember the last time I ate or if I even felt hungry. The steady Coke and Xansa diet kept my stomach feeling full. Heading over to Peyton's house I had a feeling that it was going to be a confrontation. Doing another bump at the light before I pulled up, I needed to be in a calm state when we talked so that I didn't just want to punch her in her face from the rip. The level of violence I felt towards her was crazy. It was partly due to the drugs and larceny I felt about how things were turning out. These were issues that I had that didn't reflect how good of a friend she had been to me and I had no idea of when I started to feel this way. Pulling up to the curb, I grabbed my keys and phone since I had no intentions on listening to her bull shit for too long. Rummaging through my purse I stumbled across the envelope. The contents fell on the floor revealing writing on the back of the envelope. Taking it out and flipping over the note it read:

Who will still be standing when the truth is revealed?

Hands shaking I dropped the note on the seat. What truth? Why was someone harassing me? Did someone really want to hurt me? Or my child? I was the only one in the house the night that Carlos got murdered. I hadn't told a soul about how the whole thing transpired. Peyton knew the gist of the story but I never went into details and I was too caught up in guilt and grief to even think about telling anyone else. I wanted to be free of the burden but didn't want to look like I could have prevented it from happening. Nobody wants to feel guilty about being put in a situation that they couldn't prevent. I felt helpless.

Grabbing the Coke I took another hit. Reading that letter blew my shit, this conversation with Peyton was probably going to blow my shit more. Resting my head on the seat I closed my eyes and waited.

Tap. Tap. Tap. Tap.

Opening my eyes I realized that I was still sitting in the car in front of Peyton's. The knocking was coming from her rapping on the windows. Jumping up, I looked directly into her concerned eyes. Sitting up, I adjusted my clothes and checked the time. 20 minutes had passed since I pulled up in front of her house. I must have gone to LaLa land after I took that last hit. Subconsciously I rubbed my nose to make sure no remnants remained.

"So are you just going to sit out here all day? I saw you pull up like 30 minutes ago. When I realized you still didn't come in and I seen you with your head back, I got worried. You ok?" Peyton asked while looking around my front seat. Her eyes landed on the envelope sitting on my seat with the threatening note. "Yeah, I'm good. Just got a lot on my mind. I was just resting my eyes for a minute. Here I come now." I said. Hurrying I grabbed my stuff while shoving the envelope in the glove box. Walking behind Peyton it was like I could feel someone's eyes on my back. Turning I swore I seen someone sitting behind the tinted out Town Car sitting at the corner watching my every move.

"You coming in, or watching the block?" Peyton said impatiently hold the screen door open for me to walk thru. Stepping into her living room, I'm surprised. She had redecorated and changed the color scheme. I hadn't been over in over a month even though my daughter was staying there. Whenever I wanted to see Mina, Peyton would bring her to me or I would just pick her up from school. It was cool though, I wasn't really in the mood to be around her when I was high and I had to constantly be on guard instead of enjoying my up. The face lift she gave her place brightened it up so much where before it looked like a stuffy aristocrat's house where you wouldn't want to touch anything. Now it looked like modern garden that invited you to stay for a while. It was so light and airy, I instantly felt at ease. Taking my shoes off, I walked across the cool hardwood panels until I reached the softness of the rug under my toes. Sinking into the couch, I folded my legs underneath of me and just waited to see what she had to say.

"You want something to drink?"

"Nah, I'm good. What's up? You said we need to talk."

"You know we need to talk about a lot of things. Like what is really going on with you? You're distant, doing things I would have never dreamt you do, lying to me, hiding things from me! I thought we were better than that! I thought you were my best friend, but I don't know this person in front of me. Who are you? Can the real Kennedy please stand up?" Peyton yelled.

"I'm right here. I'm still the same person, a little stressed out but the same. I'm not keeping anything from you. Peyton I lost my lover and my daughter's father all in one night. I just found out today that I was fired from my job. I know I am a mess and I need to get my life together. I'm trying." I whispered.

"You haven't even asked about Samya. Did you forget about her? Not a single word about her, you haven't called and checked on her. You haven't been to the school in a month or you haven't giving one dime to support her. Don't get me wrong, I LOVE HER BUT SHE IS YOUR CHILD! If you don't want that responsibility of being a parent anymore we can arrange the paperwork. If you"

I jumped up and pointed my finger in her face. "Arrange the paperwork? What you trying to say Peyton? Are you trying to take the only thing I have left from me? Arrange the paperwork like she is a deal to be brokered! How could you ask me something like that knowing how much I love her! I thought you were my friend! Oh I see what it is, you want my life! You want my child for yourself! You just could never be happy for me, could you?!" I yelled getting irate.

"Your child that has been living, eating, sleeping, and going to school from my house since you've been out of it. With me! I take care of her! I make sure she's warm, and clothed, and feeling loved because you haven't done it! You come in here like I owe you something, Bitch you better guess again! You got some nerve acting like I shouldn't be concerned when I caught you on your knees, fucking my dude! Yeah, I stopped past to check on you only to find Blake's bike parked in your driveway. I didn't think I was him until I opened the door using my key and saw y'all against the wall fucking. Not only were you fucking him, y'all was getting high! But how about I don't give a fuck about him, because it's always been us before he or anyone else came into the picture. You can have him and all the extra bull shit you doing. And I shouldn't be concerned about my god daughter who I love like I birthed her? Yeah Bitch, you got me fucked all the way up! I think I'm done with this conversation. Look, you're not taking Samya with you as long as you're getting high! The paperwork was so that I could take her to the doctors and sign paperwork without having to catch up with you. You think someone wants your raggedy ass life that you can't even maintain? How you going to afford to take care of her if you lost your job today? And how the fuck did that happen?" Peyton ranted. "Yeah running around here in these streets doing God knows what with God knows who. Fucking lost your job, then come in here trying to jump in my face. You lucky I still love you because I would have beat your ass coming at me sideways. Look at you all skinny, clothes falling all off! Fucking hair and nails ain't been done in I don't know how long! You look a mess! And I don't know what else your hiding, but I hope that you find peace." Peyton said looking me in my eyes. The tears just sprang from my eyes. The more I tried to suppress them the more they began to fall. I was broken and hurt. Everything she said was true and that hurt worse than anything that I had been through. The look of disappoint on her face was enough to show me that I might be burning a bridge that had always supported me. My anger towards Peyton was misguided but I had no one else to lash out at. And nobody cared enough to even say anything about the fucked up choices and decisions I was making.

"Peyton, I'm sorry. I never meant to hurt you or do anything to hurt you. I know you love Mina and want the best for her and me. I'll do the paperwork to make it easier on you; I know that you would make the best decision for her. I also know that that you would never sleep with someone that I was dealing with; I was weak and needy when he offered. I should have never said anything to Blake after I seen him in your house. It wasn't an intentional thing either. I met him the week before you introduced us. I didn't go behind your back. But I was lonely and hurt. I just wanted something to take the pain away, that's where the drugs came in. I'm just asking you to understand where I'm coming from." I pleaded.

"Understand where you are coming from? How when you keep everything to yourself? How when you've been sneaking behind my back fucking my dude while I take care of your daughter? You got a fucked up way of treating people that care about you. But you know what, Karma is a bitch. And that bitch is coming for you. I'm staying out your way. If you want to stop past next week, I'll have the paperwork for you to sign. Now please leave before I do or say something that I can't take back." Peyton said holding the front door open.

Leaning in for a hug she was as stiff as a board and unyielding when I wrapped my arms around her. I felt defeated as I grabbed my stuff and stomped past her to my car. She was right, I was holding shit in and not telling anyone what was going on with me. Not only was I hurting myself, I was hurting everyone around me. It seemed like everything I touched got broken or fucked up. Yeah, I had a cluster fuck of shit going on with no idea how to fix it.

I was trying to raise my daughter, which I hadn't done since her father got murder. So she lost two parents because I mentally couldn't deal with seeing his face in her every day. I was jobless, that meant no income. I had someone threatening my life with plans of revenge. And I couldn't admit to myself that I had a drug problem. I was on a slippery slope that was leading me down a dark hole of destruction with no idea how to dig myself out. Just as I reached for my purse to take something to take the edge off my phone beeped. Looking down I see that it was a message from Samina's grandma. It never even dawned on me to call and check on her, she went through the pain of losing her only son because of me. I hadn't seen or spoken to her since Carlos' funeral. Today, all of my selfishness was catching up to me.

MomMom: Kennedy, I have been calling and texting you to no end.
I have not heard from or seen my grandbaby. I want to see her.
Me: Hey Maria, I'm sorry I haven't responded. I have been
caught up. I promise to bring her this weekend. Are you ok?
MomMom: I'll be better when I see my granddaughter. I'll be
expecting you, and have her call me so I can hear her voice.
Me: Ok, I'll have Peyton call you so you all can speak.
Love you see you this weekend. I'm sorry

Taking a deep breath, I looked up at Peyton's house to see her watching me in the window. I waved as I pulled away from the curb. The conversation didn't go the way I expected. I thought we were going to come to blows after everything that I did to her. I guess our friendship was closer and less destructible than I thought. I was grateful for that. Racing through the streets I couldn't wait to get home so that I could get high. That was my main focus to take my mind off everything.

Tomorrow.

Tomorrow I'll find another job.

Tomorrow I'll report the letters to the police.

Tomorrow I won't get high or drink.

Tomorrow I'll bring my daughter home.

These were the thoughts running through my mind as I drove towards my house. As I approached I see a white Benz parked in my driveway that I vaguely remember seeing at the bank. My heart started racing, was this the person leaving the notes? Two figures sitting in the front seats made nervous, the coke made me paranoid. Pulling up to the neighbor's house I didn't know what to do or that was sitting in my driveway. Grabbing the Mace on my keys, I crept up to the car. Approaching the passenger side of the car I hear the familiar laughter of my sister.

"What y'all bitches doing over here? Scared the shit out of me posted up in my driveway!" I screamed.

"You told us to stop past tomorrow but we were bored so we came today. Come and cook for us." TaTa said looking at Shania. Shania was just shaking her head up and down like hurry up! Walking up to the door to let them in it was a note taped to my front door.

Sheriff's Notice
3rd Notice

The following residency will go up for sheriff sale on September 22 due to taxes not being current on the property. Please make arrangements to make a payment plan or pay the balance. If this is not handled in a timely manner you will have to vacate the property by October 18.

Clutching the paper to my chest, I was too embarrassed to show them that I was that bad off. I had always been the older sister who had her shit together. I didn't even see the other notices forewarning me that this was happen, let alone understood how. Carlos handled all the bills and taxes. I had just sat back and let manage the money. Now I see that I should have been more proactive with the household finances. What else had Los hidden right underneath my nose without me knowing? This was another thing that needed to be fixed immediately, but I knew couldn't be fixed without money. The level of fuckery was at an all time high, and it felt like I was falling into an abyss that was never ending.

My mind couldn't even begin to organize and sort through my problems to help me get to a solution that would be beneficial to me. Folding the paper I tried to hide it before anyone else could read the embarrassing words, But TaTa grabbed it and scanned the words quickly on the page before handing it back to me.

"What the hell is going on with you? Are you really going to lose this place or is that information wrong? I knew that a time would come when that façade that you put on would crack, you always seemed to have everything together and going for you. It's hard to keep that act up and harder when you're going through something that you don't want to talk about. Mom said she hasn't seen or talked to you really since Los' murder. I understand that you are going through something, but that is why you have family. Family has your back when no one else does. You look sickly like you just don't give a fuck. Everybody goes through stuff, but you got to get it together." TaTa said looking me in my eyes. For once the roles were reversed; she was giving me a pep talk when it was usually the other way around. Every word that she had spoken was the absolute truth and I the truth was a bitter pill to swallow. My vulnerability was shining bright and I was pissed that people were getting to witness my failures up close and personal. I was at my lowest point in my life that I ever been and it was humiliating. Pouring myself a drink to calm my nerves before I spoke," Look I'm going through a lot. Carlos managed the money, even when he went away. He had all of the finances ironed out before he left so that Mina and I would be straight. I never even seen a bill, I thought everything was caught up. My mind was so gone with grief; I hadn't even thought about really paying bills until that paper came in the mail today. Today I got called in and fired from my job. So now you can add jobless and homeless with a child to the list of things!"

I was waiting for some type of I told you so comment or you never listen comment to be mentioned. I was used to it at this point, you know everyone rubbing their opinion in my face without giving me a real solution to my problems. Instead they rallied around me in a group hug they whispered assurances of help and financial freedom. I was a mess, and the words weren't registering right away. The relief that I should have felt was fleeting because it still felt like I had the world on my shoulders and the weight was too heavy to bear.

"Should we tell her why we are really in town? She needs a come up more than we do." Shania said to TaTa.

"Shut up! I told you we shouldn't be telling anybody what we do! I don't want anybody judging me and my actions. I keep telling you there is a place and time for everything." TaTa said while cutting her eyes at her friend.

"I'm just trying to help her! You're always trying to snap!"

"Snap? Bitch I haven't begun to snap yet. If you keep trying to tell my business, WE won't have any business together anymore." TaTa said while waving her hands around.

"How you figure Li? You don't have that type of clout! I'm just as beneficial as you!" Shiana said with a challenging glare in her eye.

"Bitch because I'm the one that brought you in."

It was like watching a ping pong match with these two arguing. It got to a fevered pitch and I couldn't deal with the bickering anymore.

"SHUT UP!! BOTH OF YOU! You come to my house then bicker over who knows what and I am not in the mood. I need a solution or silence so that I can think. Now either you have a way that I can get some money, you're going to lend me some money, or a way to pull a caper and get the money. If not I need y'all to roll cause I'm in a horrible mood." I said.

Looking at each other, TaTa exhaled and just started talking a mile a minute. The story that I was listening to was as outrageous and outlandish as a movie script. If I hadn't seen them with my own two eyes I wouldn't had believed it.

They were high class call girls. They came back to Atlantic City, not to visit but to be arm candy on some wealthy congressman that wanted to show off for his campaign advisors. All they had to do was escort him and his assistant to several parties and meetings over the course of two weeks and would be compensated handsomely. The "company" they worked for provided them with room, board, transportation and meals. These were separate charges from the fee of $1,500 for each appearance they made with them. He had them in a Benz for a rental, gave them a credit card to shop, and kept them with any drug you can think of. Not street quality drugs, but top shelf high grade narcotics. My mind was in overload trying to mentally calculate how much I could make if I did take that path to get my life back on track. Even if my morals decided to show up, I couldn't discount that I could make a lot of money in a short time.

Daydreaming and scheming, my reverie broke when my glazed over eyes focused on the sight in front of me. Placing a mirror and a rolled up $100 bill on the counter, TaTa pulled out a bag of that unicorn dust. Making a couple of lines, she leaned over and inhaled the powder up both nostrils. Tears pricked at the corners of her eyes as she handed the straw to Shania. She followed suit and rubbed the residue on her gums. It was so casual, without any prompting that I could tell that this was normal for them. My mouth watered thinking about the rush that followed the inhale and I wanted to feel it. They both looked at me sheepishly, finally aware that they were getting high in front of me not caring whether or not I agreed. How did they know that I wouldn't freak out? Or were they aware that I had been getting high for 4 months and Coke was my favorite drug of choice? Without thinking I grabbed the bill and sniffed the 2 lines of Coke like an appetizer. It was just enough to take the edge off and make me yearn for something more. I needed something stronger and more potent. Maybe I was too used to the cocktail of drugs that Blake was feeding me and just doing

Coke wasn't getting me to the point where coherent thought were just a memory. Taking a shot straight from the bottle, we passed it around while Shania started rolling up some Haze on the counter. Turning the radio up added fuel to the fire and we started having a real party. As I consumed more drugs the thoughts about the day vanished and thoughts about being down with whatever these girls had going on was super appealing.

"You want to work with us Kennedy? You can make a whole month of income in one day, sometimes in an hour. It just all depends on how far you're willing to go. Just think you get to travel on someone else's dime for free. The hours are good but the pay is better." Shania said as she passed me the blunt. "At this point anything is better than nothing. I can't afford to live without some type of income and I want to bring my daughter home. If what y'all are telling me is true, this would be a blessing in disguise." I said.

"I was wondering where Mina was. I haven't seen her in forever! I miss her little face." TaTa said.

"Mina has been staying with Peyton until I get my shit together. All the bull shit with Carlos made it hard for me to be able to care for her. I can barely take care of myself, that's why when Peyton said that Mina could stay with her I let her. Now Peyton acting like she's the parent and I'm the God Mom! Speaking of, let me text her now and tell her to call Carlos' mom so she can talk to her grandbaby." I said, stepping out the kitchen so I could have some privacy. Walking up the steps towards my bedroom, it was like going back in time. Seeing Los' basketball shorts peeking from under the bed was all it took to take me back to that place. I could hear Carlos' voice as clear as I could hear the girls downstairs laughing. Sitting on the edge of the bed, a single tear trickled down my cheek. Wiping away the tear I couldn't help but to think about the affect my decisions had on the outcome of my life. I missed my old life and its simplicity. It seemed as if yesterday things were on the up and up. I was working and taking care of my family, all of that was wiped away in one night. I wished that wishes were true, because I wished so hard that everything would be ok. But I knew in my heart of hearts that it would be a long road ahead trying to get back to the old Kennedy.

Sending my lover was in jail for murdering my boyfriend was never in the plans. Me and Jimmy had something special; I would never want to ruin his life. Just like I thought that I was helping by telling Jimmy that Carlos wanted to rob him. I thought they would probably fight with the fist, and be mad at each other; I never thought he would shot him dead on the spot. Now the ripples of this event extended way farther than just the two people involved. Why? Is the question that I couldn't get a sufficient answer that would satisfy my need to understand? Looking down I realized I was holding the phone and Peyton had text back saying she talked to MomMom and arranged to drop Mina off on Saturday morning for a visit. I sent her a text to thank her and tell her I would call her tomorrow. The way that things were going made it hard for me to feel wishful for the future, that maybe there will be light at the end of this dark ass tunnel that I was trapped in. Because feeling around in the dark gets you nothing except holding on to the wrong thing thinking that it was something else. That's how my life felt at the moment, like I was feeling around trying to feel better but ended up feeling worse. But I was a fighter, survivor, and hustler; I just needed to get my focus back. I needed to solidify some things and get moving I the right direction of being free from my life of dependence. The steady stream of drugs, alcohol, sex, money, and Peyton all had me strung out. The drugs kept me up, the alcohol kept me down, the sex kept me yearning, and Peyton was the enabler that gave me the opportunity to have free time to explore all of these vices.

Tomorrow is what I was thinking when I heard my doorbell.

Tomorrow I'll kick my habit.

Tomorrow I'll get my daughter back.

Tomorrow I'll find a job.

Not expecting anyone, my sister beat me to it and was standing in shock as I Blake and his two friends walked. Racing down the stairs I walk into all tall, lean sex appeal and masculinity taking up the foyer. TaTa had finally gained her composure and asked who they were.

"This is Blake, and these are his two friends Kyle and AJ. Meet my sister Tasha; we all call her TaTa and my friend Shiana." I said wrapping my arms around his waist. I could see the girls sizing them up to see who would get who for the night. "Can I speak with you for a minute?" Blake said leaning down kissing my neck. Looking in his eyes I could see that he had already taken something, he was already lit. Grabbing my hand he hurried me into the downstairs bathroom, shutting the door behind us.

Pressing my back to the door he kissed me like he missed me. His hands were everywhere, the feelings turning my thoughts to mush. Everything else that was of utmost importance only moments ago were non-consequential when our bodies touched. Wrapping my legs around his waist I could feel his dick right at the apex of my cunt. Grinding my center into his, I was beyond horny. It was crazy how he could make all my circuits fire at once, and I couldn't tell where my feelings separated from my emotions because with him, they were one in the same. Placing me on the floor he lifted my dress up exposing my bare ass to the coolness of the sink counter.

"You went out all day without panties on?" Biting my lip, I just nodding my head because no words could form between my lips in fear of the moan that I felt would come out and echo off the bathroom walls.

Dipping his finger into my crease he could feel the sticky moisture gathering on the tip of his thick finger from my arousal. He lifted his finger and put it in my mouth savoring the flavor that was uniquely me. He moaned as the flavors of lust burst across his tongue. Leaning down he grabbed my leg and put it over his shoulder, looking up at me with lust in his eyes he says," I've been thinking about that flavor all day, I just want a taste. Let me and we'll go back out there in a minute." I had no clue why he was asking me, knowing that I was always down to get licked on. Words were had long been lost when he pressed his lips against mine, all I could do is nod my head up and down, praying that he would just do it already, stop talking about it! Kneeled in front of me, he watched me as he parted my lips and stuck his tongue inside the warm, pink tight channel. The smell of arousal was so potent that it was an aphrodisiac that made his need to taste me almost carnal. He licked, nibbled, kissed, caressed, stroked, and rubbed my pussy until a fine sheen of sweat formed across my forehead. The orgasm that threatened to rip through me was so intense that my whole body hummed in anticipation. His quick appetizer was turning into a three course meal with my pussy as the main course. But every time I thought he was going to let me cum, he backed off to give me a chance to simmer until I damn near burned. He knew how to play my body like a fine tuned cello, stroking my strings to produce beautiful sounds. I was so close that when he hooked his finger inside me at the perfect angle, dam broke that separated the earth from reality. The sob that tore from the pit of my stomach echoed off the walls of the small bathroom. He reached up and covered my mouth with his hands, shushing me. Telling me to let him do some things to my body, to not hold back but don't scream. The words felt like hot fudge pouring over the perfect vanilla cone, he had enveloped me in desire. All the while he planted soft kisses on my inner thighs, caressing the skin sending shivers through my already quaking body. "Dang babe, when I say sssshhhhh, you hold that shit! You screaming so loud, I'm sure everyone knows what we were doing. I missed you so much, and once I seen you didn't have any panties on, I had to see for myself." Looking up at me through hooded eyes, he watched me in the mirror, went to rinse his mouth while I could barely stand on my shaky legs. I still hadn't come down from the first orgasm yet, and I still wanted him to fuck me now. He knew what I wanted that's why when grabbed the back of my neck and forced me to bend over, I was already moaning.

Expecting him to fuck me hard, I arched my back in anticipation of the deep penetration that usually happened when he started getting rough. Instead, he just teased me. Slow, shallow languid thrust in my dripping cunt, my hips moving to their own rhythm in sync with his thrust hitting my spot every time. He was meeting my aggressive moments with patience, never letting me control the rhythm of our love making. Holding my hips, he was working on his own speed. Controlling the depth and speed of his strokes was sending me one a way trip to a small death. "Hold still and take this dick. Take what you asked for!" Blake said in my ear. The words coming out his mouth made me wetter, made my core clench. Relaxing into the stroke, he dominated me. Slow at first then frantically pounded me from the back. Every stroke felt like it could be the stroke to take me over the edge. The whole time he fucked me, he said freaky shit. The combination of two had me moaning with every stroke or dirt thing he said. Blake talked shit and fucked me. The words and stroke became too much making me scream out when he finally let me release my orgasm hit. Muffling my screams he went deeper making me cum again just as his nut came erupting out of the tip of dick. Spurts of cum landed on my ass and ran down my leg mixing with my cum until a puddle formed at my feet. Weak and sated, he turned me around and gave me his tongue. Even his kisses made me feel like I could cum from it. He never said a word as he looked me in the eyes, he just started the shower.

"I have company, we already been in here for like 40 minutes. We need to hurry before they start knocking on the door. My sister is super nosey!" I said stepping under the spray of the shower. Stepping in behind me, he lathered up a sponge with body wash and washed me from head to toe. He never said a word as he took care of my sensitive body. Grabbing a towel out of the linen closet he wrapped me in it and did the same.

"Go, get dressed. It'll only take me a couple of minutes. I'll go downstairs and entertain them to you come back down." Blake said kissing my forehead. Racing down the hall to my room, I catch my sister looking thru my closet.

"What are you doing in here?! Why are you looking thru my stuff? You have more than enough clothes." I said. "I was looking for you until I heard you scream and speak in tongues! Damn, he must be a beast for you to dip off as soon as he walked in!" TaTa said with a huge grin on her face.

"We haven't seen each other all week. He said he wanted to talk but as soon as I closed the bathroom door he attacked me! I ain't going to front, I was horny as fuck! Usually were here by ourselves so it doesn't matter how loud we get. And the things he does, makes me forget about everything else. I didn't know how long I was going to be able to entertain knowing that I couldn't fuck him right away. Sometimes you gotta get yours before it's too late." I said while I looked in my closet for something to wear.

"He seems like a nice guy and his friends are fucking sexy as shit. I want Kyle, Shania was all over AJ as soon as she seen him. Hurry up so we can party some, we can talk business later." TaTa said.

"You do know that these are not like the people you deal with for work?" I asked

"I know! I'm just trying to fuck him for my pleasure!" she said sticking her tongue out heading back down the stairs.

Throwing on a maxi skirt and tank top, I pulled my hair into a messy bun. I could the sound of laughter and music. Glasses clinking together and the sweet smell of some fire bud. The party was in full effect while I was in the shower. Walking into the kitchen, I never expected to see the scene in front of me.

Shania was on her knees with AJ's dick in her mouth. She was all into like she was getting paid with her dress pulled down exposing her young perky breast, she rubbed her nipples as she took him to the back of her throat. She must have been doing the damn thing, because his eyes rolled back in his head as he let out a roar that could shatter the windows. Grabbing his dick out of her mouth he shot all over her breast and face. Shania stood up like it was nothing, grabbed a paper towel and wiped away his essence. Holding out her hand he handed her a stack of bills. She adjusted her shirt and walked off to the downstairs bathroom to clean herself up. TaTa was just as bad or good depending on what your perception of morals was. On my living room floor she had Kyle straddled, riding him in slow motion like old lovers rekindling an old flame. Breast heaving with every stroke, she rode with her eyes closed like they were in private. Turning around I went back in the kitchen to make a drink and find the weed that I smelled when I was upstairs. Twisting one up as I drink my Grey Goose and Pineapple, I sat in shock. I had never been that open to have sex in front of people. But to be honest, it was a turn on to watch someone else in the throes of pleasure. My voyeuristic side was curious to see what brought someone else to their knees sexually. It had never crossed my mind that being watched or watching someone engage in pleasure would make me just as horny as if I was engaging in the act instead of watching it. Obviously my sister and friend are way more openly sexual than I ever imagined them to be. It didn't bother me as much as I was jealous of them having that kind of confidence and freedom in their bodies. Blake came in and sat across from me, his eyes telling me he still had sex on his mind. Sliding a pill and a baggy across the counter to me with a grin on his face, he was ready to party now and so was I. He always seemed to have sixth sense about my emotions and needs or when and what I needed to take the edge off. Handing him the blunt that I just took a pull from, I did a line and popped the pill. Taking a sip of my drink before I spoke, he just watched me. He could tell the exact moment when the drugs took effect because you could see the look of bliss across my face. But before he could speak, everyone else walked into the kitchen. 8 eyes looked at me expecting me to flip out on everyone, instead I just hit the remote to turn the music on and grabbed more glasses. Fuck it, life was short and unexpected. You might as well live it up while you had the chance. The drugs had the desired effect to give me the "I don't give a fuck!" attitude that everyone else around had adopted. They were all grown, if they decided to fuck for money that was their life and decisions. If everyone wanted to get fucked up and party, who was I to judge them when my shit wasn't even straight? Instantly the mood turned jovial and festive, nobody was here to judge anyone because we were all doing the same thing. Weed was burning, alcohol was consumed, and coke lines were sniffed. The conversation was all over the place, sometimes serious and sometimes silly. That's what happens when you put people of different ages and background together and add a chemical stimulant. So after a couple of hours everyone was ready to do 1 of two things, fuck or sleep. The company had distracted me from thinking about any of the problems that had been plaguing me, I was grateful to not have that hanging over my head even if it was only for a brief moment. All of my problems had been put on a temporary hold and it felt good. I wasn't ready to go back to worrying so I fucked Blake until I fell asleep on his chest. I would figure it all out in the morning.

CHAPTER 6
A Day then a Wake Up

"Hey I just wanted to let you know that I am going out of town this week to take care of some business. I want to come and see Samina before I go. Is that ok?" I asked Peyton as I threw clothes into my suitcase. "You have a key, and why would that be a problem you know you can come and see your daughter anytime." Peyton stated. "I just wanted to make sure first. I mean me and you haven't been on the best of terms lately, and I know it's always an open door policy with Samina being there. I'll be over in like an hour, I have some things that I need to do before I leave." I said as I grabbed up all of my hair and skin accessories.

"Ok. Oh and while I have you, MomMom called for Mina yesterday. She wants to keep her for a few days, I told her no problem. I already packed her bag; she'll be visiting with her cousins all week. She was super excited to be around other kids."

"Ok, she'll have fun. You need a break anyway and this gets her grandma off my back. So let me go and finish getting my life together. I'll give you my travel details when I get there. Later." "Later." Peyton said.

Just as hung up the phone TaTa strolled in my room holding a cup of coffee. The girls decided to stay at my house since it was late and we had partied into the wee hours of the morning. It wasn't safe to be out on the streets driving high and drunk. This morning after the guys left she broke the whole situation down for me. We were to travel to New York and meet the oil prince of Dubai and his son. The instruction stated to "escort" them to several business meetings for the week. They would pay us each $2,000 and day, put us up in the Ritz Carlton, and give us a shopping allowance so that we were dressed appropriately.

"You really don't have to do anything that you don't want to. Just know that this is the big leagues. Remember they are paying us top dollar to be arm candy. They expect secrecy and discretion. I'm sticking my neck out for you since my boss hasn't met you yet. While in NYC, we will have a meet and greet with her. She's nice but don't test her. Its serious consequences if you fuck with her, her money, or her clientele. So you think you can do this?" TaTa said over the rim of her coffee cup.

I could feel her uneasiness in her tone. I don't know if she thought that I wouldn't be able to do what I was asked to do or if I would just flake and back out at the last moment. See here is the thing, when your back is against a wall and you see no other way out, you act accordingly. And according to my bank statement, my eviction notice, and my drug habit, this was the only option. Taking a deep breath I answered with certainty, "Yes, I can do this. I have never made you look bad, if anything it's been the complete opposite."

Looking down at the incoming text on her phone, she started smiling. "I just got our itinerary for the week. This is one of my favorite clients! Not only is he stacked, he's handsome and so is his brother. He's sending his private jet to pick us up! I mean I have flown first class, but never private!" TaTa squealed.

Even though I had butterflies of anxiety about the whole thing, it was hard for me to not to be excited about going to NYC in luxury. In my mind we were going to drive, I mean it's only a little over two hours away, but I could see the perks of working for this company already.

It seemed straight forward with a lot of opportunities to make a lot of money.

"Well, my bags are packed. I have to go see my baby before I leave. You want to come with me?" I said doing a last safety check knowing I would be gone all week.

"Nah, you know me and Peyton ain't never really been friends. I tolerate her cause she's your friend. I would love to see my niece, but I'll wait until we come back. I told mama I was going to stay here for like a month to help out. I'm about to go over to Shania mom's house and make sure she's ready. Call me when you're finished and I'll pick you up." TaTa said.

Leaning in to hug my sister, I squeezed her extra tight and whispered, "Thank You, you coming here was a blessing in disguise. I swear I was up Shit's Creek with no paddle and didn't know what I was going to do."

"Don't thank me just yet, let's see how this week goes and we can talk about long term when you meet La Jefa Puta. She is the only one who can say whether you stay or leave." TaTa said pulling back from me.

Looking at the time, she grabbed her purse and walked out of front door and glided to her rental. I waved as she pulled away from the curb. Looking down I see two envelopes sitting on the foyer floor. Reaching down to get them my hands began to shake out of control thinking about what I held in my hands. Flipping them over so I could see the sender, on was from the Supreme Court, the other letter was unmarked. Standing in the doorway, I slipped my finger between the papers holding the envelope closed freeing the flap. Opening the envelope I had received a summons to appear as a witness for the state in the murder case of Carlos. In all its legalese, it basically stated that either I testify against him or get tried as an accessory since I knew details about what was going to happen but didn't prevent it from happening. I could face criminal charges and go to jail if I didn't cooperate. My head started pounding thinking about the grueling task ahead of me. This situation was just dragging on and on draining the life out of me every time it was mentioned. It was as if every time that I attempted to move on from it, something always happened to rehash it. I was supposed to show up for a hearing to give a statement and I was supposed to go in front of the Grand Jury to prove that Jimmy killed Carlos out of premeditation. That wasn't what happened at all! I didn't know what to do or say without getting into trouble myself but I couldn't let him get more time because they believed he planned the murder out. It would be up to me to show that it was spontaneous and accident that went too far. That was the least I could knowing that if I had never dated him, he wouldn't be in jail now fighting for his life. My head immediately started to spin and my stomach started to feel sick to my stomach. On my hands and knees, with sweat pouring down my neck, I dry heaved but nothing was in my stomach to come up. Tears ran down my face thinking of having to face him in court. I didn't do anything wrong but try to warn him about Carlos trying to rob him. Now it seems that I would have to pick a side even though the lines of right and wrong were blurred. Jimmy made it his own business to go crazy and kill him. Why and how did I end up in this situation I thought as the dry heaves subsided and my eyes unclouded? Resting my head on my knees I caught a glimpse of the other envelope. Before I opened it I already knew what it was. It was the same non-descript letter that I had been receiving since Carlos murder. Opening it, black roses petals swirled around the entry way. This time it was different though, the writing was the same, the sentiment was the same, but the words were different. I don't know if the previous taunt was better than the current, either way the words shook me to my core.

Time is such a Fickle thing,

It's never Enough

Sooner rather than Later

Tick, Tick, Tick, Tick

I read the last line over and over. What did they mean about never being enough time? Enough time to do what? I held my breath and just sat and thought about it for a minute. I still was no closer to figuring out what this person wanted or was talking about. Basically they were saying my time was up, but up for what I had no clue. Now there was an invisible deadline hanging over my head that I didn't know when it would expire.

At least an hour had passed before I snapped out of my stupor. My mind was trying to process the madness going on around me but found no solace in it at all. The who, what, when and why were all still unanswered questions that I had no clue how to even find an answer. It was like having pieces to a puzzle but none of them matched, something wasn't adding up. Looking at my phone, I saw that I only had another hour before TaTa was picking me up. My to do list was a mile long and getting longer the more I procrastinated trying to figure out whom had it out for me. I switched gears and made getting to Peyton's house and spend some time with my baby girl before I left my number one priority. Grabbing my bag, I set the alarm, checked the stove, and checked the windows. Locking the door behind me, I raced down the driveway to my car. Looking for a tissue, I found a rogue Xanax and enough Coke to do a line. I liked the mixture of the upper and downer, it made me mellow out. Reaching around the floor I found a half a bottle of water, popped the pill and did the line. Pinching the bridge of my nose my head lolled to the headrest as the Coke instantly hit my system. Focusing through watery eyes, I flipped down the visor so I could check my face to see if anybody would be able to tell I was on. To me, I looked the same as always, to the outside world I looked disheveled and sweaty. I didn't have time to really be concerned because I was on a deadline and didn't want anyone to be waiting because of me. Wiping my brow, adding some gloss on my lips and pulling my shades down, I hurried to Peyton's house.

• • • • • • • ● • • • • • • • •

As I approached Peyton's house, the sight that greets me is crazy. After Peyton caught us and confronted me about it, I figured she let him go. I mean hey, he was still coming to my house blowing my back out at least twice a week. He never mentioned him and Peyton's officially calling it quits and I never asked about it, but the way Peyton's mouth was set up, it was nearly impossible to think she never said anything to him about it. That's why seeing his bike at her house had me on edge. Even though he wasn't my man, we had been fucking for over 4 months; we didn't owe each other anything, so I had no expectations from him. What we had was an understanding or at least I thought there was. Grabbing the bag of clothes that I knew Mina needed from the house I sauntered up to the front door like I was a model on the runway. If they were watching, especially Blake I needed to make a grand entrance. Being petty, I used my key instead of ringing the bell. Walking in, my presence in not felt immediately, but I do hear deep male laughter and my daughter squeal like she was in a state of hilarity. Watching the scene from the kitchen doorway, my heart hurt, and I was insanely jealous of how I seen them interact as a unit. They looked like the family that I once had and had lost. Blake had Mina lifted over his head making silly faces at her, while Peyton stood back and watched while she stirred whatever it was she was cooking on the stove. From the outside looking in, it looked as if they were the perfect little family waiting to have dinner. The look of pure joy on my baby girl's face when Blake said something else to make her fall into a fit a giggles was priceless. I stood there just watching them taking in the scene. I felt like an intruder or like I was watching something private without permission, it was like another dagger in my heart. Clearing my throat the trio turned and looked me like I shouldn't be here invading they're private family moments. But what Peyton and Blake needed to realize that Mina was my family, not theirs. It was like I sucked all the air from the room and the temperature dropped 10 degrees. Mina ran to me and hugged as tight as her little arms could squeeze. It felt so good to have her back in my arms; her hug was like a salve on my broken heart. Looking up at me, I couldn't help but pick her up and squeeze just as tight. She smelled like sweetness, love, hope all wrapped in one.

"Mommy, I'm so happy to see you! I talked to MomMom yesterday. I'm going to have a sleepover with her and my cousins! Come and look at the picture I drew of us! And guess what else, I know how to spell my whole name and I know my birthday!" Samina said all in one breath and no pauses between. "Ok baby girl! Show me everything!" I said. The happiness radiating from her was contagious, and I couldn't help but feel elated to be in her presence. I missed my baby. Her kisses and hugs felt like home. Her little body pressed against me and her arms wrapped around me feel like it was no place I would rather be than with her. Glancing back as I was being lead to see her art I caught a glimpse of Blake. He watching me and Peyton was watching him. Giving him a small smirk he did the same. I knew both he and I would have a problem, or Peyton would have a problem with him when I left. But you know what, whatever problem they had was theirs. I just wanted to spend some time with my daughter before I left. I needed to love on her and feel loved unconditionally back. I made my mind shift gears so that I could focus on the great thing in front of me and not with all the extra bullshit going on around me. At that moment it seemed like the world tilted on its axis and everything that I thought I knew was wrong or different. I was confused as to why he was here in the first place if Peyton said they broke up because she believed in our friendship over a dude. But by the way he interacted with Mina I knew he was around often enough that he knew how to make her giggle uncontrollably. Whatever was whatever, I couldn't worry about that now. I focused on to Mina telling me all the names of her teddy bears, and put Peyton to the back of my mind. Soon, very very soon she would see.

Walking hand in hand into Peyton's old office, I noticed that she had completely redecorated it too, to create a little girls paradise. Candy striped pink and white walls with all white heavy wood furniture took up the space. A book shelf sat in one corner overflowing with kid's books and baby dolls. Pictures of princesses and unicorns decorated the walls. The pink and purple comforter matched the pink and purple curtains covering the windows. A cork board ran the length of the room with Mina's drawings overloading every available inch. Peyton had converted this room for baby girl to make her feel comfortable. It gave me mixed emotions about the things that Peyton had did for my daughter. It was comforting to know that she loved her enough to make her feel at home, and jealous cause it seemed like she was trying to out mother me. I couldn't help but feel a tinge of resentment that Mina might not want to leave Peyton's house.

"Come on Mommy! I want to show you all my pretty pictures!" Mina squealed as we walked over to the wall over flowing with drawings on top of drawings of us. Her and Carlos; her and me; her; me and Carlos. Looking closer I realized that she gave her dad wings in every picture. Its different how innocent a child's mind worked, she only knew the best side of Carlos. I was okay with that and sad that she was dealing with his death better than me. Guilt will do that to you. The tears immediately started to flow as I moved from picture to picture.

"Mommy don't be sad. Daddy is an angel now. He is heaven with God!" she said while her wise eyes told me she really believed that.

"Mommy knows baby, sometimes I just miss him so much that it hurts. But every time I look at you I see him right in front of me. Even though he left us, he's still here, in our hearts." I said as I kneeled at eye level so that she could see my face.

"I miss him too Mommy. I miss you mostly and my room at home. I love Aunt Peyton, but she's not you. When can I come home with you Mommy?"

"Soon baby girl. I have some things that I need to fix first. You don't like being here with Aunt Peyton?"

"I love Aunt Peyton but I love you more."

"What about Mr. Blake? He seems like a nice guy."

"Momma he is! He always jokes with me and brings me stuff. I like him, but what I like the most is how happy Aunt Peyton is when he comes over."

"That's good to hear. I'm sorry I haven't been around like how I'm supposed to be."

"Mom, I love you no matter what!" she said wrapping her arms around my legs.

"Mommy is going on a business trip this week. Speaking of, which one of these pretty pictures are for me? I need something to brighten my days while I'm away from you. When I come back, things will be different, better. I promise. Are you excited about spending time with MomMom?" I said as I watched her try to find the perfect picture to give to me. I wanted her to forget about the bad for the moment and just be happy. So I changed the topic, on to happier subjects.

"Yes! I can't wait to see her! And my cousins are supposed to be there too. We're supposed to be having a huge sleepover. It's going to be so much fun. I wish you could come with me mom."

"It's ok baby. Spend some time with your family; they miss you just like you miss them."

"I found the perfect one! I made this for you last week but I never got to give it to you."

Looking down I see a picture of Me, Mina in the middle, and Carlos with his angel wings. Even though it was drawn by a toddler, you could see the potential in her skills. And the picture was perfect, we all had smiles and we all looked happy.

"I love it! It's so pretty! You're so talented! Thank you baby, I really do love it!" I said as I examined the picture closer. Leaning down I kissed her hand as we lay back on her bed. In a comfortable silence we watched as the shapes danced across her ceiling from the night light in the corner. I knew that the next week was going to be extremely hard, but to make sure that my daughter was straight, I would do anything.

We laid there for a couple of hours, me listening to her jump from subject to subject; it was comfort in just hearing her voice. Just as she was about to go into another story on how her and Peyton went shopping at midnight, my phone pinged alerting me to a text. It was TaTa.

TaTa: Hey I'm not trying to rush you, but the town car is at Momma's waiting on you. He said we need to be at the airport in about an hour. So hurry, but don't rush. XoXo TaTa

Me: Ok, let me kiss baby girl and I'll be on my way.
TaTa: Ok, see you soon. And kiss my niece for me.

Looking up from my phone I see Blake standing in the doorway watching our interaction. The smile on his face said that he was surprised that I was such an attentive mother since Mina had been with Peyton for so long. See he only got to see one part of my life, the side that was all play. But when I was with my daughter it was all love and hard work. It felt like all my good had been put into her tiny body. I had to admit to myself that I had completely slacked off on my responsibilities as a mother but that didn't change the fact that I absolutely adored her. I sat back and let Peyton handle it while I tried to get my life and thoughts in order. I knew that I was incapable of being a positive influence over her mind, so the best I could do was allow someone that I trusted to step up and take my place. But now I see that it was time for me to suck it up and do right by my daughter by any means necessary. Grabbing Mina and putting her on my lap I squeezed her as hard as I could. Inhaling her scent and just taking in her warmth, I wish all my troubles would just fade away. Looking into her face I knew this was probably going to be one of the hardest "See you later!" that I ever had to do. But momma had a job to do, and this might be the only thing that keeps me from losing everything.

"Baby girl? Mama has to go out of town for a week. While I'm gone, have fun visiting MomMom and your cousins. Then in 3 days after you come back to Aunt Peyton's house I'll be home. I promise to bring you something nice and special back. Is that ok?" I asked my daughter who had always been wiser than her years.

"Mama, I know that you have business to take care of. I love you Mama and I can't wait to see what you bring me! Is it ok to call you every day?" she asked.

"Of course baby, of course. Now come hug me so that I can still feel your arms even when we are apart." I said

And as the moments until me walking out the door wound down, Peyton and Blake left me alone to love on my child. I knew holding her in my arms that my life was worth fixing for her, she deserved it. With every fiber in my body, the urge to bring my daughter home was stronger than ever.

CHAPTER 7
Toast

Sitting in a private jet is like being in a foreign country where everyone caters to you. Plush tan leather interior with deep bucket reclining seats, individual flat screens over each seat, surround sound, and an attendant hovering over your every word waiting to tend to your every need. I had never seen or been a part of something so opulent. As I sipped my third glass of champagne, I couldn't help but to look around in awe of my surroundings. Looking to the left of me I seen Shiana engrossed in an Eric Jerome Dickey book, across from me TaTa was flipping through the latest Cosmo magazine. I had never flown private so I didn't realize that the flight would be so quiet, I should had brought a book along to occupy me and not think so much. It was a short flight so I wasn't really worried about being bored, but I was anxious. Resting my eyes, I let my thoughts wander. I had an idea of what I was getting myself into, but not the full details. So while I was pondering what was about to happen, these hoes was unbothered. This was a cake walk for them; they had done this several times with several different men. Thinking about being sexual for a stranger had my stomach in knots. I knew what would take the edge off and make everything easier, even though I knew I should have a clear mind when I had my initial meeting with the boss. TaTa never mentioned a policy about drugs or alcohol. I didn't want to lose the job before I even had it. Even as these thoughts crossed my mind, I knew I would be as high as this jet by the time we landed. Grabbing my purse from the side table I went into the bathroom to powder my nose.

Stepping into the bathroom, I was more impressed with the bathroom than with the whole jet. Marble lined the walls creating shelving that looked like it belonged in a mansion. Double sinks under beveled oval shaped mirror, with a faucet that made the sink look like it was going to overflow. Next to the toilet that also had a bidet, was a walk in multi-head walking shower with fogged glass doors. Lavender scented reeds filled my senses as I stepped into the room making me feel instantly calmer. Rummaging through my purse, I found what I had been seeking, unicorn dust. Pouring a little on the counter I grabbed my license to make a line so I could gain a peace of mind. Leaning over the line I inhaled the substances while pinching the bridge to stop the burning sensation. Tilting my head back, I could feel the post nasal drip and the affects of the drugs almost immediately. Head lolling from side to side while a sense of peace washed over my body made the excitement dwindle to a flicker of interest. Wiping the tears that tried to escape down my cheeks, I checked my appearance in the mirror. I looked tired and in need of a serious makeover. I hadn't really slept well in a while, between the letters, the drugs and late nights, I was running myself ragged. My skin was clear, but gaunt. My hair was still long and healthy, but I needed a trim and style. I had loss some weight; it wasn't enough for anyone to be alarmed though. I still looked good, just tired and in need of a long vacation. It was nothing that the right fit, some make up, and some coffee couldn't make fabulous. Looking at my reflection in the mirror to make sure my nose wasn't dirty when I went back to my seat; I knew that today was going to be a good day. Everything went off without a hitch, so it made it easy for me to try to relax some before we landed. As I started back down the aisle towards my seat I hear these two bickering under their breath. I couldn't make out the full conversation but I did get pieces that told me that it was something serious that they wanted to discuss with me but didn't know how to approach the subject. Mumbled phrases like "Just tell her, she has a right to know", "Stop being a punk", "You should have told her already". Standing between the two I just asked,

"So what the hell is the big secret? And tell me before I hop back on the bus to Jersey as soon as this flight lands." Looking at each other Shiana just sucks her teeth and rolled her eyes before looking back down at her book. Looking at TaTa she avoided making eye contact with me; I grabbed her arm and forced her to look at me.

"Tell Me TaTa!"

"See what the fuck you started?! We could have landed first before I had to tell her the rest. But no, you're going to make me tell her now. You were so adamant about telling her, why don't you tell her the rest?" TaTa said while glaring at Shiana.

"That's your sister, you invited her. You need to be the one who tells her what the real deal is." Shiana stated matter of fact like as she grabbed her purse and went behind another door that lead to a private suite and closed it behind her. My sister grabbed both of my hands as I sat in the seat next to her.

"What?"

"First let me say, I never said sorry about not being there for you when you needed me the most. I was selfish and I was only worried about me. I should have been there to help you with my niece and support you. Will you forgive me?" TaTa said.

"Of course I forgive you! You're my sister and shit happens. Sometimes we get so wrapped up in our own bullshit that it makes us hard to be there for anyone else. I mean I was angry and alone but I really didn't take it personal. I knew that you had business to take care of. I can't expect everyone to drop everything because I'm fucked up!"

"Your right, but you're my sister. And I know you would have dropped everything and came to my aid if something like this happened to me. I should have done the same, just know I have your back. I thought you were mad that I was across country while your life was falling apart. But I have something else I have to tell you about this trip." She said while averting her eyes.

"What?"

"Well you know how I said we work for La Jefa Puta? Well she takes 15% of what we make off the top. The money is paid directly to her and then distributed to us. We are all aware of the rates she charges and what our cut will be before she sends us out. She demands a finder's fee of $1,000 to even give you a job. I know that you are super strapped for cash so I'll cover your first $1,000. I didn't realize how bad things were until I snooped in your mail you left on the counter at your house. I know I should have told you earlier but I thought that it wouldn't matter. Now I see how you need every dollar." TaTa said.

"So I have to pay this woman %15 percent off my total wages because she get's the jobs for us? What is she a Madame?" I chuckled.

"Yes and no. She doesn't sell pussy, she procure girls to escort wealthy men on trips and provides a certain level of discretion. Sex is not necessarily expected, but may come up. It all depends on the client. La Jefa's policy is to make the client a happy as possible by any means. Those means vary based on the needs of the client. She doesn't take easily to disappointing a client." TaTa said fidgeting in her seat.

"Ok, I understood that before we left. I knew that it might be more than just escorting to make that type of money. I'm a grown woman; I know what I am getting myself into. I understand the consequences if I don't follow through."

"No, I don't think you understand. If La Jefa thinks that you are being deceitful, lying, or taking business on the side there are severe consequences. Like torture and murder type consequences."

Wiping a tear from her eye she looked away as if in deep thought. "One of the girls that used to work with us, Stacy, we called her Satin. Anyway Satin got a little too close with one of her regulars and started bashing La Jefa and her ways. About how she did all the work and she shouldn't have to pay her. He started slipping her more money than La Jefa knew about. Somehow she knew that she was getting shorted. First she just disappeared, I thought she quit and went home permanent. We all say a certain amount of money in the bank and we'll quit, but once you start touching the kind of money we make and living this lifestyle it's hard to go back to a rinky dinky 9-5. So I'm on a job in a hotel laid up in a hot tub when the news report came on.

"25 year old woman, identified as Stacy Marshall from upstate New York was found dead in her bed. She was tortured and burned. She was found lying on a bed of hundred dollars bills. The coroner doesn't have an exact time of death but she was last seen two days before at an upscale dinner party on the arm of the Tax Commissioner of NYC. No details on why this happened or who did it."

I knew at that moment that La Jefa had murdered her over a couple hundred of dollars. Not because she was broke, but because she didn't like to lied too or stolen from. That's why I'm asking you now, are you in or out? It's not just about you, my niece to think about. And she's ruthless and cunning. She will go to any extreme to prove a point." TaTa said with a tremble in her voice. She was nervous and I could see why. This woman sounded like the devil reincarnate. TaTa felt like she was dragging me into something crazy and illicit. She didn't realize that even though she was the link that put us together, I would probably be involved in something way worse to get out of debt. It just so happened that she had another way for me to come up that I was willing to entertain. Either way I would have needed an immediate solution to my mounting financial problems.

"Li, I'm straight. I would never do anything to hurt Mina or MaMa. I love them to death and over. I just need to make enough to get me out of this bullshit with my taxes and mortgage. I need to make a little more to tide me over until I find a new gig. I'm not looking for longevity just some stability. I promise to be on point and never make an enemy out of La Jefa." I said standing so we could hug. Our sisterly moment was interrupted by the door opening in which Shiana had entered when we started talking. Her gown flowed easily around her feet, hair, makeup, shoes, and accessories all on point like she had a stylist hidden back there. Sitting back in her seat she looked at us both and smirked. She figured the conversation went left instead of right, but she was wrong. We may not agree on everything, but we always had each other's back.

"I told you your sister wasn't cut out for this. You know I told you that before we even got on the jet. Now what she going to do all week with no money? You got to pay her way." She said with an attitude.

"Firstly, don't get fucked up Shiana. Secondly you don't know shit about me or my life. You only know the little snippets that Li reveals to you from time to time. I'm a go getter and hard worker. And by any means my daughter will be taking care of in a safe and healthy environment. Mind your fucking business about me and mines. Don't worry about how I will make out because I damn sure ain't worried about you!" I screamed as the attendant came from the front to find out what the commotion was. "Is everything ok? Do you ladies need anything?" the stewardess asked.

In unison we all turned and said no. "Well we will be landing in about 20 minutes. I need you to put your seatbelts on and turn off all electronic devices as we ascend to the tarmac." She said in her professional voice.

Sitting across from Shiana I could feel the animosity rolling off of her. I couldn't understand why when I had never even given her second thought, let alone been a hater. Bitches love to be in your business, not knowing that you will get fucked up talking shit to the wrong one. Whatever her problem she needed to solve it and solve it quick because I wasn't beat for no bitter ass hater. I wasn't in NY on a social visit. I was here to make that coin not friends. She could either speak on it or leave whatever was bothering her alone cause that little rant she just had went deeper than this job. My situation had her thinking she had the upper hand, wrong again trick. Strapping in I sat back and rested my head. This chick was trying to blow my high with her antics. It was all good though, she was TaTa's friend, not mine. I didn't like her, but I tolerated her for my sister. But I could feel an undercurrent of hate that wasn't there before which I didn't have the patience to worry about fixing. It's cool though, if I had to whip her ass to show her to not play with me, so be it.

• • • • • • • ● • • • • • • • •

Arriving at the Trump Towers NYC in an all black tinted out Escalade, let me know that I was really dealing in the big leagues. I assumed that we were going to meet the client, but was pleasantly surprised when they told me we were going to meet La Jefa first. The high from the jet bathroom was coming down and I started to feel anxious. I was worried and nervous about meeting this woman who was so ruthless but also held my fate in her hands. If she didn't like me I was heading back to Jersey with nothing and no plan on how to get myself out of the mess that I was in. Grabbing my compact out of my purse I checked my appearance. I still needed some sun, my hair was still limp, and my nails were ratty from just not giving a fuck. But my figure, even a little gaunt, was still bad enough to turn heads. I hoped that she could see past the surface and see what I could be once I got myself together.

"Hey we're here Kennedy. First let me tell you a few things about La Jefa's expectations. She likes her girls to have a certain level of perfection when they are out with clients. She has a whole salon and spa that caters to just us located where her apartments are. We have access to those too. Everything is free to us. She will do an assessment and she will talk to you about being on the team. Just be honest about your answers because she has a knack to be able to tell when you're being less than truthful. The last thing you want is to end up on her bad sad." TaTa said as we pulled up to valet in front of La Jefa's penthouse. All the while Shiana sat with her back to me looking out the window with her lips pulled in. She tried to act like she wasn't listen, but I could tell she definitely trying to get the drop. I'll escort you up to her floor but no one is allowed around while she talked to new girls. I'll be on the floor below the penthouse. La Jefa owns that floor too. It's used as a closet, salon and a home to the girls when they are NYC instead of staying in a hotel. Someone will bring you downstairs when you're finished. Then you get all beautified!" She said as she hugged me.

Stepping out into the muggy NY weather, the sounds of the city bombarded you to the point of overwhelming you. Standing there I felt like I was a universe away from the life I just had 4 hours ago. The doorman greeted us and took our luggage as I was escorted up to the penthouse suite for my meet and greet with the new boss.

"Excuse me; can I stop in the ladies room first?" I asked the security detail before we reached the elevator.

"Yes ma'am. You can wait and use the bathroom upstairs, it's up to you?" he said from behind his dark shades.

"I prefer to use this one. I've been holding it for a while. I didn't realize that traffic would make the trip from the airport another hour long." I chuckled as I grabbed my purse and stepped into the bathroom.

Rummaging thru my purse on the counter, I checked to make sure that the stalls were all empty before proceeding to dig into my bag. It was reckless of me to try to get high right before meeting this woman, but the urge was just too strong to ignore. I really wanted to pop a pill before I went up but I knew it would take a while for it to kick in. Snorting another line of Coke, I wiped the residue across my gums getting the full affect was immediate. It was like a calming effect took over my body and I could relax. Now I felt like I could ace this meeting and solidify my spot. Breaking the pill in half, I sipped from the faucet to take it down. It was risky, but it was worth the feeling I got when I put them together. In front of a mirror already, it was an easy decision to fix as much as possible before I went upstairs. I hadn't had time to do anything else after leaving Mina besides head start to the airport. Blowing my nose to remove any residue, I splashed my face with cold water to tighten my pores. Running a damp brush through my hair, I put it up in a messy bun. Taking out my Mac lip glass I smoothed it over my lips, followed by some bronzer on my cheeks for color and a little mascara to make my eyes pop. In 5 minutes I made myself look more presentable. Surveying my appearance I was proud of the rush job that I had just completed Just as I smoothed over my clothes; I hear a quick rap on the bathroom door.

"Is everything ok in there miss?" the security guard asked through the door.

"Yes, I'm just finishing up. Give me a couple of minutes. Sorry for holding you up." I said as I swiped all the makeup into my purse. Dropping a couple of drops of Visine in my eyes and a piece of gum I was back in the lobby heading up to the penthouse.

My expectation versus what I really saw was completely unexpected when I finally met my new boss. As we approached the 37 floor the security guard pulled out a key that allowed the elevator to continue to the last two floors of the sky rise. Turning the key the elevator proceeded up two more floors with ease. As the door opened I thought we would be entering a hallway instead of directly into a living space. And this living space was nothing like I had ever seen before in my whole life. And I was super impressed.

Deep mahogany wood floors combined with the white walls and furniture made the space look chic and upscale like being in a boutique in Paris. Fluffy white area rugs covered the areas under the furniture giving it a warm inviting feeling. I immediately wanted to take my shoes off to see if the rug felt as soft as it looked. All stainless steel accents brought the whole design together in a way that made you believe that an interior decorated picked out the pieces. I could see priceless pieces of art hanging on the wall and Italian sculptures lined the doorways. Someone had paid a pretty penny to make this place look so put together and I couldn't help but look around in awe. Stepping off the elevator I could hear soft reggae music playing from invisible speakers. A complete wall from ceiling to floor was all windows opening to the New York skyline. The view was a piece of art all on it's on, but that wasn't what caught my attention. It was the beautiful brown skinned woman standing next to window who caught my attention. Draped in a long white Grecian style dress, she commanded attention without saying a word. Petite and curvy, skin the color of milk chocolate, with long wavy hair cascading down her back she could easily pass a teenager. By the curve of her hip and how she presented herself, you knew she was older than 20. Her gaze penetrated my soul and looked straight past my eyes making me feel vulnerable. The wisdom in her eyes made me feel like was looking into the eyes of woman who had seen and done things that I could never imagine. Eyes that said she had many stories untold and a cool calmness that made me uneasy. I'm not sure if it was from the stories of vengeance that I had been told or the fact the Coke had me paranoid.

Standing in the foyer taking everything in, she looked expensive like she belonged in this environment. And like a Queen on her court her minions rallied around her waiting for their orders. She surveyed me, my appearance my demeanor. What felt like forever was really on about 3 minutes, half of which I spent with my mouth hanging open in sheer wonderment.

"Everyone out! I have private business to attend to. Please sit." She commanded in a sexy accent that may have been Caribbean or Latin. In two seconds flat she had the room was cleared. The silence was so complete that you could hear a mouse piss on a cotton ball. Even though I was a good four inches taller than her I still felt intimidated about her. She exuded an aura of royalty and I felt compelled to fall in line or be subjected to cruel and unusual punishment.

"Can I offer you something? A drink, food, smoke?" She asked sitting diagonal to me on the sofa. It seemed like a trick to see where my mind was, I was afraid I pick the wrong thing and that could seal my fate.

"No I good right now. Thanks for asking."

"Well let's get down to business. They call me La Jefa Puta, that's because I am the boss who is also a Bitch. I run an organization of high class women whose attributes are endless. We provide escorts and dates for dignitaries, worldwide leaders, tycoons, and multi-millionaires. All of our clients are rich beyond your wildest dreams and expect a certain level of quality and discretion in exchange to have a gorgeous woman on their arm. We never take pictures unless asked and we never accept money unless it is done through the company. Gifts are okay as long as it is not monetary and still need to be reported to your house Ma. Before every date or trip you are to come here first and get pampered. We provide you with the means to make sure your skin, hair, nails are immaculate. We provide you with an allowance for clothes and shoes. All you have to do is show up prepared to do whatever is required of you. Some of our clients have preferences that we try to adhere to; others only need an arm piece for an event. The key word in all of this is loyalty. Be loyal to me and I'll be loyal to you. We can make a lot of money together if you think you have what it takes." La Jefa said as she circled the room talking out loud like she had did this spiel a thousand times over.

"Any questions?" she asked standing in front of me.

"Umm, maybe a few. I don't want to offend you. But how old are you? You look really young. What will happen if I don't agree with something that I don't agree with? And will I be required to have sex with these guys?" I said in a whisper.

A sound so pure, light and airy floated up through her chest when she laughed. It was music to my ears and startling at the same time.

"I'm 34 years old. I feel 65 years old and look like a 20 year old. And for your other question, you don't have to do anything that you don't want to. We screen our clients before hand to find out if that is what they are looking for first. If that is the case we tell you before you go and let you decide if that is what you want to do. Beware though; there are consequences when you don't follow through with the agreement. Is there anything that I should know about you Kennedy?" she asked with her piercing glare.

"Yes, I have a daughter who is 5 years old. Her father was murdered by my ex lover and now I'm trying to find my way back. This is my last ditch effort to see if I can make a lot of money in a small amount of time. I have serious bills that need to be taken care of immediately that is affecting my livelihood. At this point, I would do any and everything to get my life back on track, so no worries on whether or not I will follow through. I will, I promise." I said to her with a look of contrition on my face.

"Your sister told me you were going through tough times. She also said you were beautiful and determined. I see she was right in her initial assumption, let's hope that she's right about how determined you are. There is a lot of money to be made if you're willing to do what it takes.

If you have no other questions, go downstairs and get ready for your date. Since this is the first time sending you out, I'm giving you an easy client. He only wants an escort to several business meetings and Gala's while he is in this country. It should be a cake walk and you'll walk away with at 10 thousand dollars in your pocket at the end of the week. How does that sound?"

In my head I did a mental calculation: I could pay my back taxes, mortgage, and bills. I would still have money left over. That was after only working one week, this was a no brainer!

"It sounds great! I really appreciate this opportunity and I promise to up hold your company's reputation. Thank you." I said humbled thinking about how that money could almost fix everything besides my addiction.

"You can go. Oh and Kennedy, cut the Coke. I can tell a user from a mile away because I used to dabble. You're a pretty girl; don't go down that slippery slope of drug abuse. A lot of girls never come back from that." La Jefa said turning back towards the window as if in deep thought over the conversation we just had.

"Ma'am?" La Jefa assistant said as if just appearing in that spot ready to escort me to where I needed to be. We got on the elevator and she inserted her key to allow it to move to the rest of the floors. I just couldn't believe that it could all be so simple. My mind was throwing around a thousand questions that I probably wouldn't get the answers to anytime soon. Getting paid to be arm candy without any strings attached? How did she know I was doing Coke, did I residue on my nose? How did she end up being a boss of such a lucrative business? Would she know if I was skimming off the top? Stepping off the elevator in deep thought I didn't immediately notice my surroundings. At first glance you got the feeling of being in an upscale exclusive designer shop and salon. Opening to the salon was a waiting area draped in deep burgundy, a stark contrast to the clean lines of upstairs. Thick brocade velvet fabric lined the corridors, over gleaming hardwood floors. Portraits of half naked women every couple of feet made you feel reminiscent of a brothel but there was not one man in sight. Everywhere you looked you could see women of all shades, shapes, sizes and ethnicity speaking or giggling in hushed tones. Every single one of them more gorgeous than the last with bodies that was damn near perfect. The space felt jovial and open with everyone just hanging out, it seemed like no one was actually doing anything. But after a couple of minutes I noticed the doors opening and closing with women coming and going in different stages of undress. No one looked at the other with malice or hate, everyone had a common goal here: To get money.

"Ma'am, if we go to the right you can get a main, Pedi, and your hair styled. To the left there is a masseuse, a clothing closet, and an apartment that you can use. Let me show you around first and then you can decide what you want to do first. La Jefa said you would need to be ready by 9pm; you have about 4 hours to do whatever you please. I would suggest getting your hair and nails done first cause a lot of the girls come in around 8pm to get ready. If you get caught in the rush you might be late. You're allowed to pick whatever you want to wear, la Jefa keeps it stocked in different sizes. You're only allowed one outfit and pair of shoes a month for free, you can borrow as much as you want but it must be returned within a week, dry-cleaned for the next girl. There is a makeup artist on hand too if you prefer someone else doing your face, there is a personal chef on this floor too. All you have to do is walk to the kitchen, someone from the kitchen will bring the food to you once it's finished. Do you want your own space or you want to share with someone?" she asked. I was overwhelmed to say the least all I could do was nod yes.

"Yes you want your own space or you want to share?" she asked again. Just then my sister walked up, "She'll be staying with me. Thanks Stacie for everything." TaTa said dismissing her. With her hand under my elbow she escorted down the hall, as we passed women she spoke to some and waved to others. Closer towards the end of the hallway she pulled out an electronic key and inserted it into the locking mechanism to open the door. Shutting the door behind us, I sat on the edge of the bed trying to take it all in. My life had been so different 48 hours ago, now I was embarking on a new phase that was scary and exciting. But before I could even process everything going on in my head, TaTa started grilling me about my meeting. I told her it was uneventful, but she kept prying. I told her it was nothing to tell and that we should start getting ready for the night. My focus was on getting this money; everything else was irrelevant at that point that wasn't getting me paid.

· · · · · · ● ⬤ ● · · · · · · ·

Walking back to the closet, I just wanted to get a feel for what they had to offer. I had my luggage so even if I didn't like anything that they had, I was still good. The first thing I spotted was the perfect white bondage dress with a sweetheart neckline to show off my cleavage. Instantly, before even exploring I knew that I had already found my fit. From where I was standing they had a little bit of everything under the sun! Looking through the shoe selection I was in heaven. So many shoes with only two feet had me lusting over every pair my eyes could focus on. Settling on a gold pair of strappy stilettos that made me legs look miles long, I was really ready to get this evening started. I asked the attendant if she could hold what I picked out until I came back and made a final decision. I would get my sister to help me figure it out since she knew exactly how I should dress. Heading back to the room I was sharing with TaTa, I noticed a welcome basket with scented soaps and bath bombs. Reaching inside I found a hand written note:

Kennedy,

Welcome to our family. I hope that you can make all your dreams come true. Don't forget, I'm always there for you if you need me.

XOXO
La Jefa

It's the little things like this that I could get used to. After all of the other perks of working for her, I never expected her to be so thoughtful as to send a hand written note. Grabbing the vanilla scented body wash and lotion I walked into the bathroom. Turning on the sound system that was controlled by a hidden panel in the wall, I popped a Xanax, I wanted to be cool, calm, and collective for whatever I was about to witness. Sipping from the faucet I washed the pill down, and made a mental note to eat so that I wouldn't feel sick later. Undressing and standing under the spray of water, I felt like a 1,000 hands massaging away the stress of the day. If you would have told me a week ago that I would be in NYC getting ready to escort an oil tycoon around for the week I wouldn't have believed you! My oh my, how circumstances and places can add clarity to situations you couldn't see being up close and personal with what's happening around you. It's like finally seeing the trees in the forest. I had several problems that needed attending to immediately, but I had no idea where to start to make the best impact. Being here handled the money aspect for the time being. But there were at least 3 other major issues that being in NY, kept away from my mind. Who was sending these cryptic messages to my house? I had a drug habit that kept me from being a good parent to my child, which wasn't fair to her since I was her only parent. And how would I hold up in a disposition in Jimmy's trail for murdering Los? All of these thoughts raced through my head as I washed with the fragrant scent. The water felt like it could wash away my sins and make me whole if I stayed in there long enough. But this was only water, not holy water and I knew I had things to do to be prepared for tonight.

Stepping out into the steamy bathroom, I grabbed a big white towel from out of the linen closet adjacent to the shower. Wiping the steam from the mirror I stared at the girl in the mirror. She was the same and she was different at the same time. Mentally she felt beat down, emotionally she was tired. She looked thinner but her beauty was just under the surface waiting to be enhanced. Dropping the towel, I did a quick spin to survey how my body looked. I was still curvy, just without as much fullness as before. I knew that if I didn't quit with the drugs

I would lose more than my daughter. Losing my beauty was one of my worst fears. I was the chick that people seen from high school and thought damn she looks better now than when were in school. If that wasn't motivation enough, I don't understand what is. Donning a robe I walked back into the room to find a note from my sister that read she was getting a massage that I should go get my hair and nails ready for tonight. Looking in the closet I pulled out my suitcase. Grabbing a tank top and jeans to throw on, I wrapped my hair in a towel. Opening the door, I immediately noticed that it was way more people on this floor than when I first arrived. There were waiters walking around with drink and finger food on silver trays offering items to the ladies as they went to and fro. I could hear classic R and B being played softly in the background. The mood was upbeat; everyone was enjoying the routine of primping and pampering. I was still caught up in a whirlwind trying to gain my bearings. I figured I would listen to my sister since this was her show and get my nails done first since it took so long to dry.

Walking through the space, I could see that there were areas that I hadn't explored yet. I knew that there would be time and opportunity in the future to see everything that was offered. Opening the first door I expected it to look like an apartment, instead I was surprised to be met with an open salon area. There was a partition separating the nail side from the hair salon side. Black marble floors with floor to ceiling mirrors lined the walls giving off the illusion that the space was bigger than it actually was. 4 nail techs sat on one side behind tables while 4 spa foot baths lined the other side. You could easily see through the partition separating the hair salon from the nail salon. 3 girls were getting their hair styled while one was getting her hair washed. It was luxurious and upscale just like the rest of the floor. La Jefa had thought of everything and only demanded the best based on everything that I had seen so far. Standing in the doorway I didn't know what to do or how to proceeds until a short caramel toned curvaceous woman with head set appeared as if seemingly out of nowhere.

"Hi my name is Tawny. What services are you interested in today?" as she pulled out tablet to keep the details straight.

"I want to get a wash, straighten, and style. I would also like a mani and pedi." I said

"Ok, let me see. Ok we can do your mani and pedi first while these ladies are finishing up with their hair. Go have a seat in the second pedi chair and Lisa will be right with you. What is your name?" Lisa asked.

"Kennedy, TaTa is my sister." I said as I got comfortable a stuck my feet in the bubbling fragrant water. Putting my head back I closed my eyes and tried to remember the last time I allowed myself to be pampered. It was so long ago that I couldn't even conjure up an image. As a sigh escaped my lips, I felt the nail tech massaging my feet and legs. I just wanted to rest my eyes and mind. I didn't want to think about Jersey and all my problems. I just wanted to relax and focus on the task at hand, doing everything right so I can get this money. As a million thoughts are running through my head, I hear someone sit next to me taking up the other free spa chair. Not wanting to be rude I opened my eyes and was greeted by a pair of glowing green eyes staring back at me curiously.

"Hi my name is Kennedy. You?" extending my hand.

"Vicki, I know who you are. TaTa's sister right? You're prettier than I expected." She said leaning her chair back putting two cucumbers on her eyes, basically signaling that this conversation was over before it even began. It was cool though, because I didn't come here to make friends. I came here to make money, no more no less.

After getting my nails and toes painted in a bright blue I shuffled my way over to the shampoo bowl. The stylist suggested I get some layers and streaks to compliment my complexion. Her hands were like magic as she transformed my hair into a soft halo framing my face. She also suggested that I let the house makeup artist beat my face after I got dressed. Looking in the mirror I almost didn't recognize myself once my hair was finished. I couldn't wait to be all dressed up with my makeup done! Walking out the salon I walked right into TaTa and Shiana having an argument in hushed tones in the hall. Curious, I stood just out of sight so that I could listen.

"Keep running around here telling my sisters business and she is going to rock you! Mark my words. She don't play that shit, she's a really private person who will flip at the drop of a dime. And not for shit, our friendship won't last much longer if this is how you want to act!" TaTa said standing toe to toe with Shiana.

"You think I give a fuck about your sister or how she feels? No, I know that that is your sister but she ain't shit to me! She never liked me and I never liked her! She always thought she was better than everyone else, now look at her. She in the same boat as everybody else, she better get a grip and worry about how she's gonna pay them taxes on her house before she's homeless." Shiana said rolling her neck and waving her arms.

Before I could get from the door way TaTa had Shiana gripped up and slammed her into the wall. "Listen Bitch, I had enough of your raggedy ass mouth. Keep my sister's name and business out of your mouth! Now I said that shit, she doesn't have to say shit to you. The only thing stopping me from wringing your neck is Jefa's zero policy of fighting in the house. But best believe I don't fuck with you like that no more. That's my sister, hell or hot water, that's me. Its obvious based on how your acting your obviously jealous my sister, so that means you don't like me. After this week, I'll make sure La Jefa doesn't schedule any jobs with us together. Or friendship is done." TaTa said as she let the scruff of her neck go. Shiana crumbled to the floor grasping for air with tears flowing down her cheeks. She was startled when she seen me come around the corner, I could see the fear in her eyes as she looked up from the floor. Instead of being petty and rubbing it in her face that she couldn't beat me or my sister, I just walked past shaking my head. She just became another problem on the list of issues plaguing me. It's cool though, I already know that she not bout that life based on my little sister roughed her up. But a scared bitch is the one you had to watch out for, I would keep my eyes and ears open regarding her.

"Ayeee TaTa, help me pick out a fit for tonight." I said catching up with my sister. Hugging her I never said a word about the transaction I had witness between her and her best friend. I knew that I was the cause of their demise and didn't have a clue on how to fix it. She just grabbed my hand and pulled me in the direction of the closet. If I wasn't already impressed with the opulence provided for us, I definitely was now through new eyes. Rows and rows of designer clothes filled the space. Every style, color, brand and fit you could think of was all in one place. The far wall was covered in designer shoes and sneakers for every occasion. An attendant was available to help assist with sizes and to help put looks together. I just stood there with my mouth hanging open in shock that all of these things were giving to us. I would say for free but I knew that everything cost something. So why TaTa tried to figure out what she was wearing, I grabbed the outfit I seen earlier form the attendant and sipped my drink while she pondered.

After getting my fit for the night I was anxious to get dressed and start this adventure. Going into my purse I surveyed what vices I had available to me since I couldn't just call my drug dealer 2 hours away. 4 Xanax, like 3 hits of Coke, and an eighth of weed was all that I had brought with me. This was me trying to wean myself off the crap and get my life in order, now I felt like I needed to be in a constant state of otherness. I knew that if I didn't do something fast than Mina was going to lose both her parents, but that didn't keep me from self medicating every chance that I had. Not only that, I was on the brink of financial ruin and could be homeless if this thing didn't pan out.

Rummaging through my bag I stumbled across my phone and decided that now would be a good time to check in with Peyton.

Hitting auto dial, I kept getting a weird message saying that the number you dialed was no longer in service. That was odd, when did she change her number and why didn't she give me the new number? I just saw her a couple of hours ago before I came to NY. What happened that fast that would force her into changing her number? Dialing MomMom house she picked up on the second ring sounding out of breathe like she ran to get answer the call.

Me: Hey MomMom, its Kennedy. How are you?
MomMom: Good, just waiting on that friend of yours to drop off my grandbaby. I've been waiting a couple of hours now. She said around 3pm, its 6pm now. I tried to call her but I think I wrote the wrong number down. She'll be here in a couple of hours.
Me: Oh ok, I was just checking to see if Mina had gotten there yet. Can you have her call me when she gets dropped off?
MomMom: Sure honey, don't worry. And why don't you stop past when you get back in town. I haven't seen you in forever. I would love to just catch up with you.
Me: Okay, no problem. I'll be back in 4 days, I'll come past and bring baby girl too. I'm sure she won't be tired of hanging with her cousins. Love you!
MomMom: Love you too. I won't forget to tell Mina to call you, Bye.

Hanging up the phone I had a nagging feeling in the pit of my stomach that something was seriously wrong. The same feeling I had when I knew that the situation was getting ready to get crazy with Carlos and Jimmy. The same feeling every time I received one of those notes. Grabbing the phone I tried to call Peyton again, getting the same results as before. "The number you have reached is no longer in service. Please hang up and try the number again."

Popping the Xanax, I threw my clothes on after looking at the clock. According to the clock I only had a half hour before it was show time so I had to have my head right. My heart was hammering in my chest and I could feel the sweat trickling down my back. The need to get lifted to an elevated state urged me on. My anxiety was at an all time high, I was panicky, I was nervous, and I just wanted to not feel sick to my stomach all the time. The only solution I could see in my sights was in front of me, waiting to take me to a place where the bullshit was irrelevant. Taking out the Coke, I decided to do a line to bring me back down. Just as I leaned over to do the hit my sister busted through the door with her hair still pinned up. Quickly wiping the residue from my nose, I turned to see her staring at me.

"What?" I said trying to act like she was minding my business instead of me getting caught red handed.

"Nothing." She said as she walked away shaking her head in disgust. Looking at her reflection as she added jewelry to her fit, she looked me in my eyes as she spoke," Before you speak let me say what I need to say. You got a real bad nose candy habit. You think you're covering it up but anyone that knows you can see the difference. It's not only dangerous but costly. You still look good, but you're starting to look run down. You need to quit before you fall down that rabbit hole and can't get back up."

"Look I'm grown. Nobody has been through what I have been through in the last six months. You weren't here to help me! Nobody is dealing with the guilt and emotions over things that are really their own fault. I fucked up and the only way I'm dealing right now is with this. And before you judge me, don't worry, I had no intention on buying anymore because I want to bring my child back home. The only way I can do that is to make enough money to keep my house from being taken. Right now this money is my life line. You worry about you and let me worry about me. Cool? Cause the last time I checked I was the oldest." I said with an attitude.

Checking my reflection in the floor length mirror to make sure every hair was in place, I did a quick spin and was satisfied with the end product. My sister watched me with hooded eyes, she knew what I said was true even if I was using it for an excuse. The conversation was threatening to blow my shit but I wouldn't let that happened. I went on about my thing like I was before she walked back in. I knew she was coming from a place of love but I wasn't trying to hear that right now. I looked good enough to eat, my make up was flawless, my hair was perfect and the shoes just pulled the whole look together. At that moment I was grateful for a lot of things, mainly that I didn't look like what I've been through.

TaTa never even responded to what I said just watched her phone like I wasn't there. Whatever she was doing must have been important because it had her full attention, she started typing furiously as she finished reading. "Hey our ride is here, it's time. You sure you're ready for this?" She asked.

"I'm as ready as I'll ever be." I whispered to myself and followed to elevator.

CHAPTER 8
Him

Sitting in the back seat of a bullet proof tinted out black Bentley being chauffeured was something I had never dreamed of being able to afford let alone experience. And to think that all of my expenses were paid for and I still got paid at the end of the week. It seemed as if everything turned to shit to eventually turn into sugar. Glancing over at TaTa she was engrossed at something on her phone, I almost forgot that she has been doing this for over a year. She was used to be chauffeured around in expensive cars dressed just as tasteful to meet rich men from all over the world. I was still in shock that I was actually going through with her suggestion to take her up on this job offer. When your back is against the wall with no other options in sight it is hard to just not do whatever it takes. The decision becomes so easy, especially when you have a little person depending on you for love and support. Thinking of my baby made me compelled to try to get in touch with Peyton again. Dialing her number I got the same disconnect message. The only other option was to call Blake even though I knew it would be awkward asking him about my daughter and best friend. Scrolling through my contacts I found his number, punching the send button, the phone just rang and rang with no answer. I ended up leaving a message and asking him to call me and have Peyton call me. The nagging feeling making it impossible to sit still, my intuition told me to try someone else. The next move was to call MomMom and see if Peyton dropped Mina off, but before I could get her on phone the car came to a halt and we were being escorted into an upscale apartment building to meet the guys. Stuffing my phone in my purse, I sashayed up to the door with TaTa side by side. We looked so good that it seemed as if everyone had their eyes on us. Where she was brown, I was light. Where I was thinner she was curvier. But as soon as you looked at our faces you knew immediately that we were kin. We had the same facial features, same tilt of the mouth, bright eyes, and small upturned noses. She grabbed my hand as we stepped over the threshold and walked past the bellman that tilted his hat as we passed. Getting on the elevator, TaTa pulled an electronic key out of purse and stuck it in the keyboard to have access to the more exclusive levels of the building. All the way to 57 floor, aka the penthouse is where we were headed. In the last 24 hours I had been surrounded by a lifestyle that I only seen on TV and never thought I would experience. With ever step in this process I was amazed and stunned into silence. In my head I'm thinking I could get used to the opulence. TaTa watched my expression in the elevator mirrors and just started laughing.

"What?!" I said.

"I looked like that the first time I came here too. Nothing, you look like a happy little girl. I haven't seen your face light up like that since before everything happened. I'm happy to see that smile, but before you get too happy I wanted to tell you something." TaTa said looking down as if the words she wanted to say could be found on the floor.

"I know La Jefa said that we sell our services as being pretty, social women. But she never tells women that these guys expect sex or sexual favors at least 90% of the time. And I know these guys, brothers from the Dubai. They are not your typical Middle Eastern men. They are worldly, with a lot of money. They can afford anything and everything, money is not an object. They like to party hard and don't mind spreading the wealth if you're worthy. They treat all the girls great and even gift them with things depending on how well they maintain. I just want you to be prepared for anything." She said looking at me as the elevator felt like it was touching the clouds.

"So are these guys going to expect us to sleep with them? I kind of figured no one was going to pay that fee just for arm candy."

"If the father was here no, he is very traditional versus his sons who grew up with the world at their feet. He strictly likes to have a companion to accompany him during his business meetings and events. The sons, Ali and Faryd love coming to the states away from the watchful eye of their parents so they can do whatever they want to. Both are handsome with degrees in technology and really just want to come to have a good time in between meetings. I'm not sure what the agenda is for the week, but I can tell you it's probably going to be crazy!" TaTa said with a light dancing behind her eyes.

"I think I can handle it, as long as he ain't trying to get to freaky. Everybody has their limits, and my ass is my limit!" we both started laughing just as we approached our floor. Both of us started checking our appearance to make sure that everything still looked as good as it did before we arrived. Just as the bell chimed signaling we had arrived, I could hear the sounds of hip hop playing in the background. The elevator opened into a large open suite, standing in front of the fireplace were two of the most handsome men I had ever laid eyes on. They were the definition of tall, dark, and handsome. Deep brown skin over lean muscle that strained to bust out of the Versace suits they both wore. One had a cigar and snifter in one hand while gazing into the fire that was blazing in the fireplace. The other brother whom I assumed was the younger brother was on the phone speaking in a language that sounded melodic, but I couldn't understand a word he was saying, by the look on his face I could tell that it was a business call and not pleasure call. They didn't seem to notice us as we stepped off the elevator but I definitely noticed them. Dressed in expensive shoes that probably cost more than my monthly salary working for my old boss, they wore like some cheap house slippers. They looked more like some rich playboys versus some rich businessmen. TaTa grabbed my hand so that we were standing side by side, quietly waiting for them to acknowledge our arrival. Ali signaled his brother using his eyes, that's when he looked up and looked us over. They raked our frames with their eyes from the top to bottom. I could picture in my mind's eye what we looked like, her brown skin and my lighter skin, our bodies showcased in bondage dresses, and makeup/hair looking like we just walked out of the salon. Then you see the look of recognition flash across their faces, there was no denying that she was my sister.

"Well who do we have here?" the older one said as he walked towards us reaching out for my sister.

"I thought you might like a change of pace, I brought my sister along this time instead. Ali meet Kennedy."

"Nice to meet you." he said while looking in my eyes after kissing the back of my hand.

"The pleasure is all mines. Thanks for having us." I said in the most seductive voice I could muster. I was nervous and I felt my hand tremble a bit as I pulled away from him. The sweat on my palms was so moist; I thought he could feel it when he touched me.

"Hey Faryd! I see you all came back but left your father home. I guess while the cats away the mice will play!" TaTa said to the younger brother as she hugged him.

"Exactly! I needed some time away from the family business and had a couple of important meetings to attend here. I figured why not call one of my favorite girls up and have her escort me around town. You make us look unstoppable as a unit. And now that you've brought your exquisite sister with you, it's no way that the deal that I am trying to close will be a problem. I mean how can you focus on business while you sexy ladies are sitting across the table from them?" Faryd said while spinning TaTa in circle to get a view of her dress form the back. You could tell by the way that he spoke with TaTa that they already knew each other.

"And tell La Jefa that your sister is a way better choice than the other girl. She's way more polished. Not that I didn't like your friend, because she could do some strange things if you know what I mean. But you and your sister are in a league of your own." Ali said staring at the slit in my dress that revealed my smooth thighs.

"Well I hope I live up to expectations." I whispered feeling self conscience standing in front of them.

"Well let's have a drink before we go. Tonight is a dinner meeting and then we party! I feel like tonight is going to be a good night!" Ali said with a sexy smirk on his face.

In the back of my mind I'm thinking like, this maybe a business venture he was still sexy as sin. That would make anything that he asked me to do easier. Hopefully he wouldn't ask me to do anything risqué, because I knew in my heart I would do it no questions asked. Already I could tell that he had a way with words and the way he was looking at me made me believe that he usually got what he wanted. And who was I to deny him?

Having a seat on the couch he Ali handed me a flute of champagne that they had chilling in a bucket next to the couch. The cool bubbles hit the back of my throat and I instantly relaxed. The champagne settled some of the nervousness I was feeling. I didn't know exactly what I was supposed to be doing so I just sat, sipped and watched. TaTa went into the adjoining room with Faryd and shut the door, leaving me with my thoughts and Ali.

"You know you don't have to sit there like that. You can talk to me; I mean we are going to spend the next week together. Maybe we can get to know each other a little better before we head out. Tell me about yourself." He said sitting on the other end of the couch with the flute being held by two fingers.

"Well I'm 26 years old. I've been a personal assistant for the last 5 years up until last week. I have a 4 year old daughter and now I'm here. My life is boring, but your life seems stellar. Why don't you tell me about yourself? You seem way more interesting than me. What type of company does your family run?" I asked trying to deflect the conversation. Unintentionally mentioning my daughter brought a whole new wave of worry. I still hadn't heard from Peyton or heard from Mina. I was trying not to worry but it was hard not to when you didn't know what was going on. 12 hours ago I was just standing on her living room holding my baby girl and now the phone is disconnected. Peyton would never change her number without immediately giving me the new number. We had been friends longer than we hadn't been friends, she knew me just as well as I knew her. That's why not being able to reach her was so unusual. My thoughts were running rampant as I thought about all possibilities of something being or going wrong. Did she get hurt? Was the person who was threatening me harassing her? Is she unable to reach a phone?

"Hey are you ok? You just looked really worried and distant. I don't think you heard a word that I said in the last 5 minutes." Ali said grabbing my hands looking in my eyes.

"Yeah, I'm good. I just have some unfinished business back in Jersey that needs to be taken care of when I get a chance. I apologize, when I mentioned my daughter it just all came flooding back. But you know what, it's absolutely nothing I can do right now from here except enjoy your company." I said immediately fixing my expression to look interested in what he said.

"Well we have an hour before the driver is supposed to meet us. If you want to make some phone calls your more than welcome to use the other bedroom for privacy. I understand having priorities, even though I haven't had a chance to become a parent yet. My company is like a baby that always needs to be checked. Go handle your business so that you can be at ease during dinner." He said walking me towards the other side of the suite where his room was located.

"Thank you so much, I will only be a minute. I promise! You have no idea how much this means to me."

"You know you can always show me later." He said with a wink shutting the door behind me. Sitting on the edge of the bed I pulled my cell out of my purse to see if I had any missed calls or messages. I had 3 missed calls from MomMom and none from Peyton. I could feel the anxiety clawing at the pit of my stomach thinking about what was going on. Feeling around in my purse I found a half of a Xanax and drowned it down with the rest of the champagne in my cup. Pacing back and forth as I dialed, I checked my messages first. It was dead air where the caller hung up without saying anything. No return number or message, just dead air. I hung up and dialed MomMom to see if Mina had arrived. I was impatient to say the least, I wanted answers. I zoned out while waiting what seemed like forever for her to answer the phone.

"Hey Kennedy, did you hear from Peyton cause she still hasn't bring her yet. The number that I had for her isn't working. I don't know what type of games y'all are playing but I want to spend time with my granddaughter. I try to stay neutral but this is ridiculous. You said she could come and I've been waiting all day and she still hasn't been dropped off yet." MomMom said with an attitude.

"MomMom, I am away on business. Peyton was supposed to drop her off until the beginning of next week. We talked about it and she was excited to spend time with you and her cousins. I would never tell you yes and not bring her; she is your grandbaby too. I don't know what the heck is going on because I can't get in touch with Peyton either. I don't know what's going on but I will find out. Mina is my daughter and she goes I where I say, not where Peyton thinks is best."

"I'm sorry, I know this whole thing hasn't been easy for you, and I wasn't accusing you of anything. I was just wondering what was taking so long. I just want what's best for the both of you. I miss my son and now Mina is the only tangible piece of his legacy left. Please just find out what is going on and call me back. I'm sorry to take you away from your business trip."

"It's ok. Let me see if I can get in touch with her. I'll call you back." I had already hung up before she could even finish what she was saying. By now the Xanax had started to kick in and I could feel the mellow affects taking hold. Pacing while I tried to think, I could faintly hear the voices in the living room drifting through the door. I almost forgot that I dressed to the nines in a penthouse suite getting ready to be an escort for a business meeting. Taking a few calming breathes, I tried calling her again. Same stupid message that felt like a ton of bricks fell on my head when the operator said, "The number you have reached has been disconnected or changed. Please try again." I tried to call Blake and he sent me to voicemail. I tried to call him again, instead off answering he turned the phone off. I left him an irate message about not being able to find my daughter of Peyton, to please call me ASAP. Please! My frustration was soaring at an all time high; it seemed as if I couldn't get a grip on anything.

Fuck it, I thought as I put a line of Coke on the counter. I needed to be up and alert. Every unanswered call or message made my mood dipped. This was my only solace. That little baggy with the white crystal was the only thing that could ease my anxiety. Checking my nose I came out the room and acted as if everything was fine. My face oozed confidence and sex appeal, but inside I sick to my stomach with worry. But in the back of my mind, I knew that something was terribly wrong. I didn't know exactly what but I knew intuitively that something really bad was waiting for me when I got back to Jersey.

• • • • • • • • ● ●• • • • • • • •

Sitting in a 5 star restaurant being surrounded by money, old and new, makes you either envious or admire the rich. The potential clients that Ali and Faryd were hosting were nice, their wives weren't. The first couple that arrived was in their early 50's, investment brokers looking to cash in on the untapped market that Faryd and Ali found before anyone else. The other couple, the man was at least 20 years her senior. You could tell that she was strictly a trophy and had no goals or aspirations outside of his money. She was young and pretty, but we were younger and prettier. The thing about the rich is they always compared money. Whether it was old or new, how you made it, how diverse was your portfolio looking, and lastly can they out buy you. Coming from a poor background, being rich, whether inherited or earned, you still had money! Initially I couldn't understand the shade that was shrouding the table. Then I realized it was these two birds mad because we were there. All during dinner they kept making condescending comments about me and my sister being their girlfriends versus their wives. I took it all in stride though; I had no intentions of seeing these stuck up high siddity bitches again. They just kept making little comments about wealth and breeding, how they inherited their fortunes, or how they married into money. Like I said earlier, it didn't really matter where the money came from but that you actually had money to discuss or compare. See I was here to get paid just like they were. The difference was I was actually working for it while they lucked up and married millionaires. I was way hip to the shits, the difference is they had the chance to mingle with wealth versus me having to stumble amongst. That just made us different type of go getters in the same race. I wanted to say so bad, bitch you lay on your back every night to be able to spend your husband's money in the morning! But I knew that I would only be hurting my pockets so I kept my thoughts to myself and nodded at the appropriate times. The really sad part is I could tell there was an underlying current of hate between the wives, so instead of being enemies they were allies tonight against me and my sister. It was cool because in a street fight or war of words both of them wouldn't stand a chance against us. We were what they used to be and it was hard sitting across a table with your husband while he hung onto the young pretty girls words. So after appetizers, soup, salad, and before the main course I excused myself to go to the ladies room to touch up my makeup.

Walking into the bathroom I checked under the stalls to make sure no one eavesdropped on my conversation I was about to have. What I needed to discuss wasn't for everyone to hear, I wasn't in the mood for explanations. Going into the last stall I shut the door and pulled my phone out. No messages, no text, no missed calls. At that moment I felt like nothing was better than something. I assumed the best since MomMom didn't call me back that meant Mina was with her. When I got back I was just going to pay Peyton's bill because that was the only thing that I could think was wrong. In all the years that we've been friends we've always been in constant contact with each other. I've never, not been able to get in touch with her for more than a couple of hours. It was strange and weird. That little voice in my head was alerting me to something being seriously wrong beside a simple phone bill not being paid. The mixture of the Coke and Xanax had me zoning, where my level of awareness was well below subpar. The warning siren should have been sounding loud and clear instead my head buzzed annoying like a gnat was bothering me in my sleep. Why did Peyton always have to make things so difficult for me? She wanted everything her way or the highway. This stunt with Mina just proved how much control she thought she had over my child and what she did. Taking the Coke out my purse I sprinkled enough to do a line on my compact mirror. Snorting the line gave me the extra clarity I needed to get through the rest of this dinner without snapping on one of these old washed up bitches. The easy part was ignoring them the hard part was not letting my anxiety boil over and make me lash out over something that has nothing to do with them. Either way, it was no way possible I fucking up my money opportunity. I had to keep reminding myself that I was here on business and not pleasure. My main focus was being pleasant and looking good enough that the minute details of the deal were looked over and the deal was struck. Just two more course and we would be out of this stuffy restaurant, soon surrounded by celebrities and models in somebody's VIP drinking the best of everything. Stepping out the stall

I stood in front of the nearest wash basin so I could check my makeup. Washing my hands first, I never noticed that there was someone else in the bathroom with me. It just so happened to be the 50 something year olds wife. If looks could kill, she would have incinerated me from the feet up. The smile on her face couldn't distract me from the way her eyes shot daggers at me. Instead of feeding into her bullshit I just kept rinsing like she wasn't even there. But when I looked up I knew exactly why she was looking at me like that, I had Coke residue around my nose, and my eyes were glassy and dilated. I had a wild look about me that wasn't there before I came into the bathroom. Quickly wetting a paper towel I tried to hide the evidence by sneezing. She just looked at me ruefully and shook her head. You could see all the ill thoughts floating around her Botox filled head. I really didn't care though; I would never see this woman again. So her judgment of me was totally irrelevant. So while she watched me in the mirror, I watched her.

"You know that is a nasty habit that you need to get under control before it ruins you." she said while drying her hand on a paper towel. Her eyes never left mine as if she was waiting for me to react to her words.

"How about I'm grown and I can take of myself. It's really none of your business and I didn't ask for your opinion. Thanks, but no thanks." I said as

I touched up my lip gloss as if she wasn't even there anymore. I dismissed her with a lack acknowledgement like she had done my opinions over dinner.

"It is my business when your boyfriend wants to do business with my husband. Who he does business with affects me because he invests with my money. I am the bread winner. And if Ali wants to have a Coke fiend for a girlfriend that's his problem but then shit trickles downhill, which means me. You're a pretty girl, but I advise for your benefit you get some help ASAP."

"And I asked you what again? Oh, that right, nothing!" I said as I rolled my eyes. I was hustling to get out the bathroom before I could say something that could fuck up my money. She was already rich; she could stick her nose in anybody's business and still come out clean. Instead of there being an argument she just kept on like I hadn't just took a shot at her.

Reaching in her purse she grabbed a pen and wrote two numbers on a napkin.

"The 1st number is the number to an addiction specialist. They help you figure out your triggers and how to avoid and work through them. The 2nd number is mine, Lorena, because even though you may think that I don't like you, I do. I see a lot of me in you. Don't let whatever is happening in your life take you on a downward spiral that you'll regret later on." She said while taking the shine off her nose with her compact sponge.

"How did you know I had a problem? I'm curious?" I asked leaning on the counter to face her.

"I knew because you've been sniffing and rubbing your nose all night. Those are tell-tell signs that you sniff Coke. When I was in the thick of things, it went from sniffles to nose bleeds." She said closing her compact leaving me standing in the mirror.

Walking back out to the table I noticed that the dishes had been cleared and everyone was having after dinner drinks. The atmosphere had lightened after all the business talk was done and now everyone was trying to enjoy themselves. Almost everybody, because the other wife was looking at me suspiciously as I sat back down, she kept looking between me Lorena trying to figure out what secret we were keeping. Instead of feeding into her bullshit Lorena just nodded her head and stirred her coffee. You could tell that she was dying to ask her what happened, but she wasn't stupid enough to do it in front of everyone. TaTa was telling the guys something that had them laughing uncontrollably capturing the attention of anyone in the restaurant that was within ear shot. The distraction made it easy for me to try to fade into the black and ponder the conversation I just had in the bathroom. My palms were sweaty and I felt anxious and self conscious when I looked over at Lorena like she could see the wheels spinning in my head.

"Kennedy you want dessert or a drink? We're getting ready to wrap up and head out." Ali asked squeezing my knee under the table drawing attention back to the present. Involuntarily my body reacted and I felt the urge to squirm in my seat. The sensation was so profound that it was felt all the way to my core, the clenching and unclenching of muscles, that a sex sigh escaped my mouth. I just shook my head no and closed my eyes and tried not to think about how good his hand felt on my thigh. How could he turn me on without ever touching me intimately? How could I be turned on at a moment like this? The Coke had me feeling some type of way, and if we weren't in such a crowded place I would have had Ali right there on the spot.

Zoning out trying to get my emotions in check, I closed my eyes so I could focus. When I opened them, seven sets of eyes were staring at me in wonderment. The guys had lust in their eyes and the wives had larceny in theirs. Before anyone could say anything Faryd signaled the waitress for our check. My sister's gaze was the most penetrating of them all; it was more like she was looking through me to my soul. It was like she could see all my thoughts and feelings, but it may have just been the affects of the drugs that had me paranoid that everyone was judging me. All I could do was have an inside chuckle at the absurdity of my thoughts. Drugs, they had that type of affect on you.

• • • • • • • • ● • • • • • • • •

After the bill was settled, Ali walked with his hand on the small of my back as we went to valet to wait for our driver to pull up in the front. He whispered in my ear, "Is everything ok?" I turned and put on my most seductive face and said, "Yeah everything will be fine once we get somewhere quiet, you and me." With a wink I turned on my stilettos so he could get a good look at my ass as I stood next to my sister at the curb. In my peripheral, I could see Lorena and the other wife having a heated conversation. From what I could gather through the bits that were spoken too loud to be secret that it was about me and my sister. The surprising part was that Lorena was defending us. Telling her to be quiet cause she started from nothing and fucked her way into a rich husband. This went on for a couple of minutes before I saw Lorena roll her eyes and walk up to me.

"It was nice meeting you ladies. Kennedy, I hope to hear from you sooner than later." She said with a head nod.

"Yes, it was nice meeting you too. Of course within the next week, I'll give you a call." I said as I clutched her hand. She gave me firm squeeze before she hopped into the back of a Lincoln Town Car with her husband. Valet pulled up a Benz next and the other waved as they got in their car and pulled off.

"What was she talking about? It seems like y'all became fast friends when you went to the bathroom.' TaTa said in a hushed tone.

"We did. Let's just say she's not as stuck up as she seems. She wants to help me with what you were saying earlier. I'll tell you more when we're alone." I said.

That's when our driver pulled up to the curb in front of us. All four of us slid into the backseat and got comfortable.

"Yessss! That was an awesome dinner! You girls, you girls, you girls!" Ali said as he spun me around.

"You girls help seal the deal. I don't know what you said to Miles' wife in the bathroom, but she came back and was gung ho about her husband signing. You might be my lucky charm!" Ali said uncorking a bottle of champagne pouring glasses for everyone.

"I propose a toast! To new business deals and fast friends!" Faryd said. As the glasses clinked together and the first sip hit the back of my throat, it was the first time since we been together that I actually felt relaxed. Ali grabbed my ankles and put my feet on his lap like we had known each other for years. Rubbing his hands up my calf's all I could do was moan and lean into the feeling. My skin being overly sensitive just made the feeling of his hand caressing my legs orgasmic. I wanted him to keep going higher and higher until he could touched on the spot that really wanted to be touched. Parting my legs a little, I wanted to encourage him to keep going. I didn't care that my sister and his brother were in the car with us. I was aroused by the wealth, ambition, and authority that he commanded. And just when I thought he would continue, the car came to a complete halt. Opening my eyes, I could see that we were in front of one of the most exclusive clubs in New York. Tonight was turning into something great!

The driver walked around and opened the door for us to get out. The men stepped out first and helped us since we both had on heels and dresses. As soon as our feet hit the red carpet leading to the club entry way the lights started flashing. Even though we weren't celebrities, we were with foreign royalty. The paparazzi didn't have to know who were, our clothing reeked of wealth. Cameras flashed from every angle capturing pictures of us with our dates as we walked right past the velvet rope and straight into the club. The guys shook hands as they passed security guards, but I could see it was more to it than that. They tipped every person they encountered as they passed to ensure that we were treated like royalty. It felt surreal being on the upscale side of the club versus swishing between sweaty bodies. You could hear the deep bass in the bottom of your feet as we were escorted by a curvy red headed woman to the VIP area overlooking the club. Even though the music was loud, it was muted up here. The dance floor was packed with men and women of all color and nationality moving in unison to the beat.

Music had no boundaries and could bring enemies together if the beat was banging hard enough. Watching the club revelers from above it looked like all love to me. The way the rich party was completely different from how I partied my whole life. You actually got a chance to enjoy the company of fiends instead of people spilling drinks all over your shoes. I was amazed at how different the atmosphere was from looking at the dance floor. The VIP area we were in had the feeling of a Moroccan palace. Deep jewel tones and velvet fabric covered the round seated couches. The light gave off an amber glow that made you feel like you were somewhere exotic. In the far corner was a fully stocked bar with a bartender waiting to take our order. It seemed as if they thought of everything to make you spend as much as you had to enjoy what they had to offer. Faryd waved the bartender over and gave him our drink orders. Standing over the club it felt like I was a part of this elite group of people instead of actually working. This was play for me, so when Ali grabbed me by my waist and pulled me into him I just melted in his arms. Swaying back and forth to the music letting the sounds take me to another place. I could tell he was just as turned on as I was by the way his body felt pressed against mine. I wanted to stay like this until magic happened, but I knew that right now wasn't the time or the place. Opening my eyes I could see my sister and Faryd watching us. With bated breath, I grabbed my sister and started dancing seductively in the middle of the VIP like we were the only ones in the room. We had did this routine thousands times in clubs all over South Jersey. We knew how to command the attention of every person within our presence. Dipping and spinning, hands on her hips moving like two synchronized swimmers. Grinding on her like were lovers. Dancing together since we could both stand, that made our movements fluid like we practiced. And both men couldn't keep their eyes off of us like every woman in the room watching us enviously. As the beat switched and another song started to play, I wanted to be in the thick of things. Observing from a distance is good, but being in the middle of the crowd with bodies pressed against you was a whole new level of freedom. Grabbing my sister I started pulling her towards the door that led down to the dance floor. Looking over my shoulder I signaled for them to follow us with the crook of my finger saying follow us.

Pushing our way to the center of the club I grabbed Ali and gave him back. Grinding as close and seductive as I could get, I gave him a show. Bouncing and grinding to the music while his arms engulfed my waist and caressed any bare skin I had exposed. Where ever he touched flames erupted, kissing my neck as I laid my head on his chest. All the feel good endorphins flowing thru my body had me lit, but I wanted to feel great. I wanted to do a line and pop another pill; I was ready to take this party to the next level. As the song wound down, I decided that now would be the perfect time for a touchup. I was hot and sweaty from the mixture of drinking and dancing. Turning around to face him I put my hand on both sides of his face and kissed him like he was my dude.

"I'll be right back. I just want to freshen up." I said

"Well don't keep me waiting, I'll be upstairs." He said, squeezing my butt as I walked away. Turning to look back he looked dazed like he couldn't believe his luck. The feeling was mutual, because he was definitely a step up from any dude I had fucked with. I guess money makes you confident on another level. That confidence was a huge turn on. I figured by the end of the night he would think he hit the lottery with the way that I was feeling. Scoping out the scene a little I wanted to see what my sister was up to. Instead of finding her on the floor dancing, I found her in a dark corner entangled around Faryd like old lovers. Pulling her to the side I told her I was heading to the ladies room and his brother went back to VIP to wait. Wrapping her arms around his neck I could see her whispering in his ear. He nodded and started heading for the stairs too. She grabbed my hand as we ventured through the throng of moving sweaty bodies. Moving thru a packed club is a dance in itself, we shimmy and shook to the sounds. We passed people dancing so close they should have been naked. People kissed and made love on the dance floor. Hook up was arranged and marriages were broken. The clinking of glasses mixed with the sound of laughter and music was like a symphony to your ears. With TaTa in the lead, my hand firmly grasped in hers, she got us through the crowd in record time. Standing in line dancing to the beat, the high was calling me. I was already hype but I could feel the effects of the Coke and Xanax wearing off. I wanted to keep that euphoric feeling going, it kept my mind off other things. As the line moved, a girl kept lingering and looking around the ladies bathroom line. I already knew what was up; this wasn't the first time a drug dealer waited around the bathroom catching clients. My interest was piqued as to what she had to offer. Fuck it, I was in New York for the week, basically hoeing. Hoeing for a whole lot of money so spending the little bit of money that I had on me been a no brainer if she had something that I really wanted. So when she walked past me the second time, I grabbed her arm.

Whispering in her ear I asked, "What you got?"

"Molly." She said as her eyes darted around to see if anyone else heard.

"2."

I handed he the 20 and took the two pills. TaTa looked up and wondered who I was talking to and about what. As the bathroom cleared out and we were next I handed her the pill.

"Are you trying to roll with me?" I asked her handing her bottle of water.

Without answering or questioning she popped the pill and chased it with water. The pill was more than enough with the alcohol. I knew it took about 20 minutes for it to kick in and I couldn't wait! Freshening up we chatted and complimented the other ladies on their fit. It was all love and it felt like all love. Everyone was in a jovial mood; it was a good night to be in the company of great people. Walking arm in arm through the club back up to VIP we could both feel the effects of

Molly taking hold. First the feeling of something being wrong, then the anxiety leads the way to a feeling of freedom and self love. By the time we hit the stairs to get back to the guys I felt like I was the music. The song that they played moved through my body how blood flowed thru my veins. Any inhibitions, doubts, worries, fears faded away. The beat seemed to get louder, vibrating up my legs through the soles of my shoes. The walls pulsed in time with the racing of my heart. As we reached the top step, and I grabbed Tata's hand, we caught our reflection in the panorama mirror lining the stairs. We looked like two vixens ready to tear shit up, and the Molly made us feel like anything was possible. When we intertwined our fingers, it was like a zap of electricity traveled from my fingertips all the way to my core. The flood was immediately coming down my thighs. I couldn't wait to get my back blown out, it seemed long overdue. But I had a feeling that Ali would make up for that lost time.

Sauntering up to Ali while his back was to me and rubbing my hands up his chest, I couldn't hold back the moan that slipped from between my lips. I was horny and I was rolling. This little cat and mouse game that we had been playing since we met was about to end. See, he thought he was the cat and I was the mouse, but what he didn't realize is that he was about to get swallowed whole. Turning to face me with a snifter filled with ice and amber liquor, I wrapped my leg around his waist and pulled him closer. Dipping my fingers into his drink I grabbed the ice cube out and put it in my mouth. My movements had him enthralled, he pulled me closer and watched my mouth as I slowly let the cube melt, dripping between my breast.

"Oops, I made a mess. I wonder if someone could help me." I said in seductive whiny voice poking my lip out for emphasis.

He leaned over and licked a trail from my neck to between my breasts, collecting all the liquid that fell along the way. Pulling my dress down, he took my nipple into his mouth. My body arched up to meet his mouth while I ran my fingers through his hair. There was no space between us and yet I wanted to be closer. Hooking my leg around his legs, I pulled him closer. When our middles touched, the part where I was soft and he was hard, we moaned in unison. He wanted me just as bad if how he felt pressed against was an indication of what was to come. Backing me up until my legs touched the back of the lounge area, I let myself fall back. Just then, I looked up and seen TaTa with her dress up around her waist, breast pushed to the glass of VIP overlooking the club, while Faryd fucked her hard from the back. The level of eroticism playing out in front of me was too much for me not to watch. I had never been a voyeur, but I couldn't tear my eyes from the scene playing out in front of me. If it wasn't my sister, I might have been tempted to join them and make him into a sandwich. Ali grabbed my face and made me look at him after kissing me senseless.

"You don't need to watch them when we can be doing our own thing." Ali said while kissing me hard again.

"But I like to watch, it turns me on. Let's get out of here and continue this conversation somewhere else private. Somewhere where I can do some things to you that you won't believe." I whispered.

Taking his phone out, he made a quick call. Pulling me towards the other side of the room away from those two fucking their brains out, he pushed me into the far corner to try devour me whole. Everywhere that his hands touched felt like electricity floating through my body. The overwhelming sensation of his hands and mouth had my thighs slick with anticipation. He put one hand under my dress and felt for my wetness. Putting his finger into his mouth he tasted me off his hand. I was so mesmerized that I didn't hear the phone ringing until he said "Ok."

Grabbing my hand he kissed me and I tasted myself. I wanted him more than I had wanted any man in a long time. I don't know if it was him or the Molly but I almost couldn't contain how I was feeling. The trip to the car was like walking a tightrope, at any second I felt like I could erupt in flames. The sea of bodies pressing against me as his hand clasped mine tightly, every sensation was heightened giving a whole other level of awareness of what was going on around us. And I felt at one with everything and everyone. If I would have looked over and everyone was fucking, I would have joined in. That's how turned on I was at that point, needy to say the least. Pushing through the throng, someone ran their hand up my thigh and a mini orgasm escaped. Finally we reached the front door and I could breathe again. The fresh cool night air felt like stepping into an oasis in comparison to the heat of the club. I inhaled deeply and could feel the moisture on my skin dry up. Before I could get my bearings, I felt his hand making small circles on the exposed skin of my lower back. Getting lost in another kiss made me forget that we were waiting for the driver to pull and take us back to the penthouse suite.

In the backseat of the car I tried to contain myself. Getting two glasses I poured us a drink. The champagne intensified what I was already feeling. The bubbles felt cool in contrast to how hot I felt. The whole time Ali was just watching me with the eagle eye. I could tell that he was having the same type of reaction to me that I was having to him, the only difference is I was high and he wasn't. Or maybe he was, I just never seen him step over into the dark side. Sipping, I looked over the rim of the glass at him, taking my tongue I rimmed the glass before taking another sip followed by a moan.

"It's hot, do you mind?" I asked as I pulled the top of my dress down letting my breast be free.

"Why are you teasing me? I think we should wait until we get back to the suite. I am not as inclined as my brother to have you in front of everyone even though I am very aroused. It would be my pleasure to take you right here and have my way with you. But I will practice some restraint and wait, I have a feeling that it will be well worth it."

"Since you don't want to help me, I might need to help myself." I said tweaking my nipples into tight black pearls. Squeezing harder the pain turned into pleasure, and before you know it I was in my own zone. The pleasure made clit zing and it was almost impossible for me to stop touching myself once I started. Staring at him as I dipped my finger in between my legs, the aroma filled the backseat. I was so wet; I couldn't help but taste myself. Licking the sweetness off my finger made him moan watching me. Moaning and writhing with my head back, I was trying to spurn him into touching or fucking me or both. I didn't care! I had had enough of this little game of wills we were playing. The drugs and alcohol had me ready to cum all over the backseat by just using my own hand. I started rubbing the right spot to make me fall over the edge; we were already at the hotel.

The driver must of knew that we were doing something risqué, because he tapped on the window before opening the door. That gave me enough time to gather my wits and adjust my clothes. Ali stepped out first and held his hand out so that I wouldn't stumble. Standing on shaky legs from the orgasm sitting right on the cusp, I tried to look unaffected. Walking with my hand tucked neatly in his arm we walked start to the bank of elevators and got on. He pulled out his special key to unlock the upper levels where only the elite stayed, and where his suite was located. Looking at my reflection in the elevator mirror, my lips looked swollen from the kisses we shared and my eyes looked wild because I was so aroused. Raking my fingers over my hair to catch the fly aways, I still looked flawless. I looked like a sex vixen ready to devour my prey. Standing side by side, you would never know that I was being paid for this gig. From the outside looking in we gave off the aura of two wealthy socialites that had too much to drink and couldn't keep our hands off of one another.

The elevators opened to the suite and I was still in awe of its opulence. The lights of the New York skyline gave a soft sexy glow to the suite making lighting not necessary. Walking in ahead of him, I let my dress fall off as I strutted. Turning to face him, I was naked except for my heels and jewels. No words were needed to beckon him to me. Face to face we watched each other like this was the first and last time we would ever have this experience again.

"Hey I never asked you, do you like to party?" Ali said while his fingers stroked a melody in my middle. My focus was on what his hands were doing not what his mouth was saying.

"Yes." Was all I could manage because the wicked things he was doing with his fingers made me weak kneed.

"Before the sex gets too good, let's take a break and get right. I want to get you so far gone that you'll enjoy anything that I want to do to you. And believe me; I want to do some things to you." He said while licking down my earlobe. My mind was still focused on the sensations that he was assaulting me with that I didn't realize he turned and walked to the safe in the wall until I felt the difference in the room. I perched myself on a barstool and watched as he pulled out a large duffle bag with a keypad lock on it.

"I keep it locked up because I don't want housekeeping snooping in my things. Imagine if they got a hold of this bag, I couldn't report it missing. I would be out a whole lot of product that I cannot easily be replaced especially since I'm in the states. Now come pick your poison." He said punching in a code opening the bag.

Looking inside I couldn't believe that he would travel with this much contraband. The sheer quantity and quality of drugs was unbelievable. That's when I realized how big time he was able to get this type of stuff overseas and not have to worry about getting caught. In the bag he had any type of drug you could think of but only in high quality, none of that stepped on shit that they make you pay high prices for in the hood. He was legit with his and I suddenly got excited to see what type of trip that he would take me on. Sticking to what I knew, I decided that I would do a couple lines of Coke to get me up, a Xanax to bring it down, and some weed to mellow me out. I planned on fucking him all night and I planned on being the best lay he ever had.

My naked body covered in jewels that sparkled in the light that reflected from the NY skyline, I lie back on the bed and let the pill take effect. Meanwhile, I rolled one up and drank another glass of champagne. The whole time I touched myself, my breast, my hair, between my legs all while moaning. I knew what I was doing, not only was I trying to stoke the fire in me, but I was keeping him in high gear. I wanted to push him so far to the edge that he would beg me to allow him to enter me. Legs spread on the bed; he came and sat on the edge with a mirror covered in Coke. Taking a Black card out of his pocket he made 4 lines for us to snort. I laid there and watched as he handled the Coke like he had been getting high his whole life.

I sparked up as he lay at my feet and started touching me where I left off. My feet, calves, inner thighs, he made small feather light circles that made me moan a squirm. My back arched every time he acted like he was going to touch my pussy. He wouldn't though, he would get so close that the thought of his hands on me there and I was ready to cum. Sharing the L with kisses in between, I could feel the pill making me relax. With the relaxation came the needy feeling that I wanted him more and more by the minute. I was doing my best to turn him on while he had already made me feel like I was coming undone at the seams.

As he passed me the L to take the last hit he moved between my legs. The bud must have had him feeling some type of way because his eyes took on a glassy dreamy look. Kissing and nibbling up my thighs, I didn't know whether to tell him to stop or keep going. The whole time he kept his eyes on me, gauging my reaction to what he was doing. I never expected him to want to please me as much as I wanted to please him. Now I could see that giving me pleasure was giving himself pleasure at the same time. It felt good to think that this was about us not him or me, but both.

The contrast between his tongue and warm breathe was making me weak. I couldn't think past the sensations that I was feeling. My mind was completely focused on the pleasure that he was giving me, and I wanted more. He drove me crazy with his mouth, getting close enough to my clit that I could feel the energy float between our bodies but never touching her. When he finally put his mouth on me, I couldn't do anything but pant and squirm. Instead of running from him, I was inching closer to his mouth. Grinding my hips in wide circles to ensure that he didn't miss a spot and that he got every drop of my sweetness as it trickled out. I wanted him to lick away all my worries and pain. I wanted him to lick and nibble until my love came down and drowned us both. He stoked and stoked and stoked and stoked until the pleasure was so great I had no other choice but to come back down. His mouth did things to me that I had never experienced. The feeling of euphoria that covered me, made me want to sex him so good that we both collapsed. Kissing his way up my stomach, licking and nibbling on my skin, I was needy and I felt obligated to reciprocate what he had done to me. So as he kissed my mouth and I could taste myself, I moaned into it. Pushing him down so I could take the lead he flipped me back over on my back. He wouldn't allow me to pleasure him the same way he tasted me. He wanted to be the star in this movie. All I could do was follow his lead.

"Lay back and let me enjoy you. This is my show; I just want you to watch me." Ali said as he licked his lips like he just finished a full course meal.

Watching him move up my body, I could see his muscles straining in anticipation of what was about to happen. He kissed my face while grinding his dick into my clit. First contact made me arch up to meet his anxious thrusting. I could feel my wetness being transferred onto him making it slippery enough that he could slide right in if he wanted to. The slickness made it easy for him to glide all over my sensitive area making my cunt greedy. I wanted him to give it to me so bad but he had other plans. I think he wanted to tease me until I died from the pleasure. Until finally he thrust up and found my entrance dripping and tight. The only words that I could mutter at his intrusion were "Oh shit!" while biting my lip to keep from screaming out. I was waiting for him to punish me but he surprised me with taking it painstakingly slow. So slow that I could feel the head of his dick throb as he penetrated me deeper touching walls that felt like they had never been touched. The deeper he went the more I felt like I was going to come with every thrust. Slow and deep while he kissed me, he said freaky things in a language that I couldn't understand and didn't care because he sounded so exotic. All you heard around the suite were skin on skin, wet kisses, the sound of macaroni and cheese being stirred, and me moaning like I had never been sexed this good ever. Even with all of the wild sex and escapades that I had experienced, it had never been like this. It had never been so intimate and all consuming. I don't know if it was the drugs or I was just feeling him that made this experience so erotic. I think it was mixture of the two combined with the fact that he was filthy rich in his own right. It was too much and too many sensation that I couldn't tell where one ended and the next one crested. And when we finally connected in the most intimate way, his pelvis touching my pelvis with no space in between, I immediately came. And I came hard, with explicit words and thrashing. He just kissed me and kept stroking me at his leisurely pace while I went crazy underneath of him. Before I could get my bearings another orgasm ripped through me so hard I thought that I would shatter from the impact.

Slowly I came back down and was amazed that he took me there and brought me back without cumming himself.

"Kennedy, open your eyes and watch what I'm doing to your body. Look at me while I make you cum." He said while turning my face towards him. As I looked into his eyes I came again. He let me relax a little before he plowed into me so hard, it hurt so good. I was sensitive and weak, all I could do was lay there and take what he was giving. He was giving me the deepest, longest dicking that I ever had. All the while he fucked me senseless staring at me, whispering in my ear, sucking my neck making me wetter and wetter. He told me to get on my stomach while he stroked me from the back. Hard and fast as I tried to hold on and enjoy the ride we were on. I had already ridden the wave twice and didn't think that I could cum again even if he was hitting all the walls that never been touched. Dirty words, moans, and skin on skin contact is all that you heard over the soft music playing. Then I could feel him getting bigger and longer than he had been the whole time we were fucking, I knew he was close to losing it but was trying to prolong his pleasure. Grinding my ass in circle while he held my waist, I could feel the pressure building in my stomach signaling that I would cum again. I started panting knowing that we would cum at the same time. Just as the thought crossed my mind then he came in a rush, and the pulsating from his dick pushed me over the edge again. We both screamed out with our combined pleasure. I was ready to collapse and fall into a deep fitful sleep. Ali had other plans, he spooned me until both of our hearts stopped racing. Caressing my damp skin as we lay on 2000 thread count sheets, I could feel myself drifting into that happy place when you orgasmed too many times back to back. Ali got up and kissed my shoulder told me he would be right back. He fucked me so good that I couldn't even respond to his retreating back as he went to the bathroom. The sound of running water and soft music filled the space where moments ago you heard sounds of pleasure.

"Come and bathe with me. I ordered us a feast so we can get our strengthen back. Let's continue." He said reaching for me. My legs felt wobbly and weak, but I knew that the bath he had prepared would do wonders for my body. Pushing through the fog of sleep that threatened to overtake my overused I headed to the bathroom. Walking past the mirrors that covered the walls in the bathroom from ceiling to floor, you could tell by the light blush all over my body that someone had just been fucked well. I felt exposed and on display after being I the dimness of the room. Hands over my breasts I looked around as if I wasn't just at moment ago spread eagle ass naked in front of him. The freedom I felt when we entered the room dissipated once I started to come down. My high was wearing off and the insecurities started to manifest its self in the form of shyness. You could see every bump, bruise, or ding on my body and he just watched me as I walked over to the Jacuzzi that was overflowing with fragrant water.

"Don't cover yourself from me. You're beautiful and passionate. Is there anything specific that you want from room service that I haven't ordered? I want to do a couple of lines while we lounge." Ali said pouring more fragrant bath oil in the tub as I sunk down to my neck in bubbles.

"I'll have whatever you order, it should be fine. Bring the champagne in here too when you get the Coke. Let's stoke this fire so we can go all night." He hurried out the bathroom and brought the liquor and drugs back. Sipping from the flute while doing a bump, the jets in the tub had me nice and relaxed like making drifting off into a peaceful sleep alluring. Ali had other plans though. He changed the music to something foreign and up tempo. The sounds of twangy string instruments mixed with flutes and drums had the beat rumbling in the pit of my stomach. Unconsciously my body moved as if on its own accord. Head back resting on the edge of the tub, hips winding to the beat, I could feel the water shift as he lowered himself into the other end of the tub. Tapping my leg he took my foot into his hand and stroked my arches. But he did more than stroke; he knew the art of touching someone's erogenous zones. The way he touched me felt like he was stroking my feet and my clit at the same time. He made me cum with his hands without ever touching me sexually. Water sloshed over the edge of the tub when my body bucked during orgasm.

"Damn Ali, what are you trying to do to me? That was......
Awesome!" I said struggling to my wits about me. I felt hot and achy even though we had been fucking for hours, I should have been sore but I wanted more. The drugs had me floating. His loving had me insatiable with lust.

"I'm just trying to show you how much I enjoyed your company. Plus you have no idea how rich you've made me tonight. I never ask what women talk about, but I'm curious as to what you and Jason's wife talked about in the ladies room. Just to be a fly on the wall" He said as he caressed my ankles.

"Nothing interesting, just lady stuff. Why don't we take this party back to the bed? This water is getting cold." I said standing with water cascading down my body. It was pointless in telling him that she was going to help me kick my drug habit. Why spoil what we had going on? He followed me back to the room just as Room Service knocked announcing their arrival. Grabbing one of the plush robes off of the door, Ali donned one and hands me the other. Surrounded in warm Egyptian cotton terrycloth, I sank into the plush king size mattress and let the scent from feast he ordered invade my space. It wasn't until then that I realized I was famished. I hadn't really eaten at dinner; I was too busy trying not to blow the deal for him. Picking from the buffet that he ordered, my eyes were bigger than my stomach but I still stuffed my face. But sitting there watching him in his state of disarray, hair falling into his eyes, bare chest showcasing how hard he worked his body, I was hungry again. But this time it wasn't food. I was getting addicted to the lifestyle. The drugs, sex, money, and opulence had me in a daze wondering what life would be like to live like this daily. All my problems didn't exist to me right now. And even though it was work and I was getting paid, it didn't seem like it. This was a vacation in comparison to my last job.

Making a line on the dresser, I inhaled until I felt that familiar feeling in the back of my throat. The Coke was so pure that as soon as I sniffed, euphoria overtook my mind and body. Watching him in the mirror as I wiped off the residue, I made eye contact with him stroking himself. We watched each other, making the temperature in the room rise because of the fire passing between us. Everything we did tonight had the undertones of Karma Sutra. Ali aroused me in ways I never thought possible. Turning around, I dropped the towel and started walking toward him seductively. Leaning over the bed, I took him into my mouth. And that's when I knew it was going to be a long long night.

CHAPTER 9
Reality

Buzz. Buzz. Buzz. Buzz.

The incessant distant buzz like an irritating ass gnat broke me out of the most peaceful sleep I had in a long while. My body was relaxed to the point it was like I had a ton of bricks covering me. Trying to lift my head to see where the sound was coming from seemed almost impossible.

Buzz. Buzz. Buzz. Buzz.

The feeling of not knowing where I was or what happened last night had me feeling so disorientated that I didn't know what day or time it was. Rolling over I felt the warm body of someone slumbering next to me, it felt familiar and unfamiliar at the same time. In my subconscious I knew it was Ali, and could vaguely remember the wild night we had. What was going on?

Buzz. Buzz. Buzz. Buzz.

The sound stopped so I stopped struggling to get up. It felt warm and safe like being cocooned by the sun. Letting myself slip back into the happy abyss of sleep would be so easy, but the sound was back again.

Buzz. Buzz. Buzz. Buzz.

Finally forcing my eyes open a sliver, I could see that the opulence I had been exposed to since yesterday and was still astonished. I was far from poor but I was hardly rich. Sitting up the room started to spin, the light rushing into my head mad me nauseous and dizzy. Stumbling out of bed grabbing his button down shirt that was thrown over the ottoman I went to relieve myself. Rinsing my face and mouth I looked at a reflection I bore the marks and looks of a party girl who had a wild night. Limp hair, makeup smudge, lips and eyes swollen from the lack of sleep and more partying, I was a sight to see. It was going to take a miracle to get back looking right. I knew it would take a whole lot of water, a flat iron, and some aspirin. But I was still tired, so getting back in bed after relieving myself was like a dream come true. I said fuck it; I was too exhausted to do anything else.

As soon as my head hit the pillow, snuggled up under Ali, wrapped in that down comforter I could hear the sound again. Glancing at the clock I saw that it was already after 2 pm. We damn near slept the day away! Jumping up I realized that the sound was someone's phone ringing on vibrate. Grabbing my clutch, the purse stopped vibrating before I could see who was calling. When I finally got it out I had over 40 missed calls. My heart beat accelerated in anticipation of what I was about to hear. Nobody calls you that many times unless there is something wrong. The anxiety that I felt when I first arrived in NY was back ten times worse than before. Hands shaking, I didn't know who to call back first. Most of the calls were from MomMom, several were from my mom, a couple where from sister, one from Blake, and one from a blocked number with a message. That prickly sense that something was wrong was so prevalent that I thought I might throw up with worry

None of the calls were from Peyton.

40 calls and not one was from my best friend that my daughter had been staying with for the last couple of months. Before I could start checking the voicemail, my phone started ringing again. The number

was so familiar that it was probably the only number that I knew without looking in my cell phone.

"Hey mom, what's up?" I said trying to grasp what exactly what was going on.

"Hey, I was wondering when you were going to call back. I stopped past your house to take in the mail and I found this envelope. It didn't have a post marked on it but it had your name. There was also a box on the steps that said fragile so I brought that inside too. Should I open it since you're not coming back until the end of the week? It looks important." My mother said as I hear her tearing the tape from the top of the box.

"You're already opening it?! Sheesh, let me answer you first! It might be something in there that I don't want you to see! Go ahead! Have you heard from Peyton?" I asked while on speakerphone trying to go through all the text messages I missed. And just when I had zoned out and found a text from Blake saying to "Call me, it's about Mina" my mother shrieked.

Jumping up I started pacing, not even worried that I was naked. "What happened Mama? What was in the box?!!" I demanded.

"Oh God, it's a dead cat with a note! Oh my God, Oh my God! What have you done? It says "This cat is dead just like you are to me!" Its dead roses surrounding it! What is going on Kennedy?!" my mother wailed as she spoke to me.

"Mom, calm down. I'm not sure what is going on. But I promise as soon as I get back, I will handle it. What about Peyton, you seen or heard from her? I've been trying to reach her since I got to NY and haven't been able to. It says that her phone is disconnected."

"No, I haven't. But why would someone send something like this to you? Especially after all that you just went through." Mom said.

"Mom, I don't know but I will find out. Well let me go, I need to try to catch up with Peyton. She was supposed to drop Mina off with her other grandma yesterday but didn't yet when I talked to her around 8pm. If you hear from her tell her to call me ASAP. Love you mom, text me if you need me because I'm working. I may not be able to pickup."

"Okay baby. Be safe and I'll call you." my mother said before she hung up.

Grabbing Ali's shirt off the chaise lounge, I threw it on as I looked for Blake's number. Grabbing a bottle of water I went into the bathroom so that he couldn't hear my conversation. Who knew what this guy was about to say, but I wanted to keep my personal life separate from my work life.

"Hey it's Kennedy, you said call you ASAP. Where are Peyton and Mina? And why did she change her number and not tell me?" I said as soon as Blake answered the phone.

"Kennedy, I don't know what to say but she left." Blake said in a monotone voice.

"What do you mean she left? She left and went where to do what?" as the panic begin to set in.

"I went past her place and everything is locked up and she is nowhere in sight. When I looked in the window everything was gone. Kennedy she left and took Mina with her. I don't know where or why but I haven't seen or heard from her." He said into the phone.

"Blake if you know something, please tell me! How could she leave? Wait, did she take Mina too? Let me call you back and see if she is with MomMom." I said before I hung up in his ear and speed dialed MomMom.

"MomMom it's me Kennedy. I got your calls, did Mina get there?" I asked as I slide down to sit on the bathroom floor. The feeling of dread was slowly shrouding me, paralyzing me with fear. I had a feeling that whatever she was going to tell me was going to be the worst thing she could ever say.

"I've been calling you since last night about this. I thought you already knew what was going on; Peyton came past here last night with Mina. She told me that the plans had changed and that she had to go somewhere and took Mina with her because she wouldn't be back on Monday to pick her up before you came back. She let Mina play with her cousins for a little while and then she said they had to go. She kissed me and said she would see me soon and left. I thought you knew what was going on. I was calling because I thought you changed your mind and decided that you didn't want her to stay here." MomMom said rapidly making her accent that much more enunciated.

"MomMom, I don't know what is going on. I haven't heard from her since yesterday. I am so worried and I don't know where my child is." I said as the tears started coming down my face.

"I need to come home now! I need to be in Jersey and see what is happening myself. I'm getting dressed now and I will call you as soon as I get home." I said as I wiped my face. I ended the call before she had a chance to say anything else. Right now it was nothing she could do for me.

Something told me to check the voicemail to see who left me a message form a blocked number. Pushing 1 to activate the voicemail the message started playing.

"Hey Mama it's Samina. Are you coming soon? Aunt Peyton said we were going on a trip. I got a new doll and toys. And I ate all my food. I love you." was the entire message said. Just the sound of my daughter's voice made me feel better and sad at the same time. But that message just made it all the more clear that something was up. Where did this chick take my child? Mina never called and asked when I was coming, she loved staying with Peyton. The red flags were flying like a beacon at this point. This whole thing was all wrong, why was the number blocked? And why did baby girl want me to pick her up? Too many things just weren't adding up and I wanted answers!

It was time for me to go, it was too much going on and as of now I had no clue where my daughter was. Going back into the main suite, I could see Ali checking emails on his phone. I hadn't expected him to wake up right behind me and start working. I guess that was how he stayed rich, always a step ahead of the grind. I walked over to him and kissed his lips. For a minute the kiss blinded me to what I needed to be focused on, and that was getting home to find out what was going on. Breaking the kids, it was time to move my ass and get going.

"You seem distracted, is everything ok?" he asked as I rushed around the room trying to gather up all my stuff.

"I have a little problem that needs to be taken care of at home. I know my contract was until the end of the week. Hopefully I will only be gone a couple of hours and can come right back. I need to get in touch with my sister. Have you heard from Faryd this morning?" I asked rummaging through my suitcase trying to find something to throw on after my shower.

"I haven't heard from him yet but I'm pretty sure they are still sleep. They stayed at the club when we left. Who knows what time they ended coming back." Ali said getting off the bed. I was temporarily side tracked when I realized that he was still naked. He was even better looking than I remembered in my drug induced haze and his dick stood out majestically as he stretched. Walking towards me he put his hands on my waist and pulled me flush against his body. His arousal was so noticeable that my only option was to reach out and stroke it. He moaned deep in his throat like I was killing him. I knew that I was leaving and something in my heart of hearts told me that I wasn't coming back. This would probably be the last time I ever seen this man. He had been so good to me since we met. This is one of those times when I wish I met him under different circumstances. In a perfect world we would have never even crossed paths ever. But in this moment, in this space, it didn't matter. I needed to see if last night was a fluke or he was the real deal, plus I needed to feel good before I left because I was probably going to feel like shit when I got home. My skin was prickling in anticipation of what I wanted him to do to me before I left.

Kneeling in front of him, still wearing only his white button down shirt, I looked up into his eyes as I took his dick into my mouth. His eyes closed tight as his knees buckled when I tried to swallow him whole. I was trying to make this experience about him, he had pleased me in was that I thought impossible. I just wanted him to remember me the same way I would remember him. Thinking about last night had my coochie was trickling down the inside of my thigh. The moistness was distracting me from what I was trying to do. While holding him in one hand, the other hand trailed down to my lady parts to relive the pressure that was building from watching him. I couldn't resist moaning once I started circling my clit over and over. Eyes closed letting him use my mouth like he was fucking me, I could feel him ready to explode. I knew that if I timed it right we could both cum at the same time, him in my mouth, and me from my own hand. I wanted to please him knowing that whatever I did at this moment would probably be the last memory we shared. Just as I could feel the ripples of pleasure bubbling from my core, Ali's fingers tightened in my hair. His moans were louder, his movements were jerky cause the inevitable was about to happen. Increasing my pace, two fingers up to the knuckles while my thumb ran over my clit, my orgasm making me cry out and let his dick fall out my mouth just as a geyser of nut erupted from his tip. Thick ropes of cum shot down my chest, leaving a stain on his white button down that would probably never come out. Both of us breathing hard in our post orgasmic bliss, I couldn't move from the spot that I was sitting on the floor. Ali ended up sitting next to me, wrapping his arms around me, whispering sweet nothings in my ear, smoothing my brow. In a perfect world I could melt into his touch, but there were other things that needed to be taking care immediately.

Disentangling myself from his embrace, he looked worried.

"I know this is just work for you, but you could at least act like you like me!" Ali said exasperated. "I thought that what we had was different, special, but now I see it was all about the check. Well I hope you enjoyed yourself." He said grabbing his robe.

Stopping mid reach while rummaging thru my luggage, I turned and looked at him. In my head I was deciding, what was the best way to handle this situation without making it seem like I was running away from him? Even though this was a job, I had never done this before. I had no experience on how to treat or talk to a john after we finished what they requested. Everything about this was new to me. Should I tell him that I needed to get home because I didn't know where my child was and I had no idea how to get in touch with Peyton who fell off the face of the earth? Do I tell him this is my first "date" ever? That this is the first job that La Jefa sent me on? That I only took the job because my house was going to get taken or that I just lost my job? That I had a drug problem that was getting out of control? Or should I just keep up the fantasy of who I portrayed to be, a working girl, be who he thinks that I am?

"It's not what you think. I really like you Ali. But I know that under any other circumstances you wouldn't even look in my direction. I'm not a real working girl. This is the first client that I've ever had. TaTa is my sister and she brought me in because of some financial difficulties that I have been dealing with. I'm a single mother just trying to make it. I need to get back because my daughter, Mina, is with my best friend. I haven't been able to reach her since I left Jersey. And usually I wouldn't be worried but we haven't been seeing eye to eye lately. I've been calling her since I left and her number is disconnected. I'm frantic with worry.

It's really inappropriate to be telling you about my problems when I'm on a paid gig. I just wanted you to know so you wouldn't think I was blowing you off. I haven't enjoyed myself like this is so long. I am grateful to have a break from life for awhile; the best part was getting paid for that distraction. I never wanted to tell you but I don't want you to think no type of way about me." I said as I rolled my suitcase towards the door.

"I'm sorry I assumed. You don't seem like the type to be in this business unless it was a purpose behind it. I like to think that I'm a good judge of character, that's why I have been so successful in business. You're too classy and smart for this to be your chosen profession. If there is anything that I can do to help you, please let me know. My resources are at your dispose. I hope that all fairs well, but if not here is my contact information. I'll tell La Jefa to pay you your whole fee plus the gratuity that I'm adding. You have no idea how lucrative the merger you helped seal the deal last night did for my business. You earned every penny of it plus more. Now get ready so I can have the copter take you home." Ali said while punching in some numbers into his phone.

Closing the bathroom door behind me, I turned the shower on full blast and undressed. It seemed like I was moving in slow motion and the world was in high speed. As I rinsed my sins down the shower drain, brought a level clarity to the situation that was boggling my mind that had alluded me for so long. As the water cascaded over my head it washed away the night and made me realize a couple of the things that I neglected in my state of constant inebriation over the last couple of months.

- Peyton had been acting some type of way every since she found out about me and Blake.
- Peyton got me to willingly sign over custody for Mina because she lived in a better school district.
- Peyton knew I was dabbling with drugs.
- She also knew that I was on the verge of losing my place.

It never bothered me before that our lives were so intertwined until now when I wanted to make my own moves. Now it seemed like she had been a great friend and I had taken advantage of her when that wasn't the case at all. Any person that went thru a traumatic experience like witnesses the murder of your boyfriend would send anyone into a tailspin. It seemed that she manipulated everything and used me falling on hard times to her advantage. On the flip side, I could see the error in my ways and thinking. I could have made better decisions that wouldn't have resulted in anyone losing their life. It made me see how much of a bad, inconsiderate, selfish friend I had been to her. All she ever did was try to be there for me and Mina. All I basically did was take advantage of her and her kindness. I could have done things differently, but my actions were based in another reality. My heart hurt and my spirit was broken surrounding the death of Carlos. The pain made it almost impossible to do anything besides mask the hurt. Now I was in a state of disarray trying to find the one person who always had my back thru thick and thin.

Throwing on a pair of jeans, flats, and tee I walked back into the suite with my hair wrapped in a towel. Ali was still on the phone and IPad at the same time engrossed in whatever the person on the other line was saying to him. He lifted his pointer finger signaling me to give him a minute. The anxiety of what I was going back to was so great I was tempted to get high just so that I could deal without breaking down. Sitting on the chaise my leg was tapping out a beat that sounded like Samba it was so fast and rhythmic. My nervousness was showing in all of my movements. Checking my phone, I needed a distraction from the waiting game. Deciding that calling my sister before I left was the most pressing issue, I rang her and waited for Ali to hang up with his call. My intentions were to Call the front desk and have them bring me a car to take me back to Jersey. The money it would cost was inconsequential in comparison to me getting back to Jersey fast. It was almost a three hour ride but it beat taking the bus or train with all those other people. Ringing TaTa, I expected her to not answer immediately but she did.

She sounded wide awake and chipper. I didn't know how she had so much energy after she partied harder than me last night.

"Hey sis, how was your night? I'm down in the fitness center. You know I gotta keep this figure tight. It's my money maker." TaTa said I could hear the other people in the gym grunting and counting reps in the background.

"TaTa, I have a problem. I've been trying to get in touch with Peyton since we left yesterday. Her cell is disconnected and she never dropped Mina off to her grandmother like she was supposed to. I don't know what is going on, but I need to get back to Jersey ASAP. Can you call La Jefa and tell her that I have to leave this job, I hope that it's a misunderstanding but it doesn't feel like it." I said putting on my flats.

"I will, but I don't know how she is going to take it. She only hired you because of me and this is one of the best paying customers. You're putting me between a rock and a hard place sis. But I understand, go find out what is going on with my niece. I'll let her know. How are you getting back to Jersey?" TaTa asked.

"I'm going to order a car to drive me back; it's too much of a hassle to try to take public transportation. Plus I don't feel like being around people. My nerves are a wreck and we already talked about what I was trying to do. So that makes it harder to be around people when I'm withdrawing." That's when I looked up and made eye contact with Ali. His stare was so strong and penetrating I felt like he was peering into my soul.

Never breaking eye contact with him, I wrapped the call up telling her I would text her when I touched back down. I was ready to go and the longer I sat on the phone the longer it took me to get closer to some answers.

"So I heard you say that you need to get back ASAP. I can charter my copter to land you at the helipad in AC. I don't mean to listen to your conversation. But I can give you the contact info of a friend of mine who handles delicate situations. Give him a call if you run into any kind of problems, he's a problem solver. Big or small, he will help you at any time of day. Don't worry I told him to bill me for his services if you utilize him. Well I don't want to hold you up any longer, I have a car waiting to take you the copter. I am happy I met you, even under the type of circumstances. I hope to see you again, but if I don't Kennedy, good luck in all your endeavors. I hope that everything works out in your favor. Good Luck." He said as he leaned down and kissed me on my lips. Not an "I want to fuck you kiss", but a sweet soft kiss.

Grabbing his hands, he slid me an envelope. "Don't open it until you get home. I promise not to tell La Jefa, I know she has a strict policy about her girls receiving tips that they don't tell about. That's between me and you."

"You have no idea what this means to me, I mean everything. You have been nothing but a gentleman to me. I appreciate everything." Just then there was brief knock on the door. The valet had arrived to take my luggage. Hugging Ali as tight as my frail arms would hold him, I turned and followed the valet to the elevator without looking back. I knew that in a million years we would never cross paths again; our lives were just that different. It made me sad to think that status was what would keep us apart. His family would never accept me as anymore then someone to occupy his time, never anything more. The urge to get high was creeping back up on me full fledge. But I also knew that if I didn't attempt to be strong I was going to be in a world of trouble. I needed my wits about me if I was going to do this right. Being strong, I resisted because it was too much going on that I needed to be focused on. I couldn't see the light at the end of the tunnel.

• • • • • • • • ● • • • • • • • • •

Getting back into the back of an all black tinted out Benz, it was a short trip to the helipad. Ali was really a boss and it showed in how well the arrangements were made in 20 minutes. He had everything planned out and ready by the time I stepped back out the bathroom dressed. Even though he just met me, he treated better than some people that I knew for years. I was grateful for his kindness towards me, I would never forget him. Now all I had was time to think about my actions and unanswered questions. La Jefa would probably definitely drop me and I had no idea how my actions would affect my sister since she was the one who got me the gig. I prayed that I wouldn't hurt or disappoint anyone else that I loved; I could leave with anymore guilt. Thoughts of guilt always made my mind trail to Jimmy. I still needed to get back and figure out what the outcome would be with Jimmy and his trial. I hoped that for his sake they would rule it as a self defense case. For my sake I hoped the same, so that at least it would be one less person angry with me. I would hate for two lives to be over because of me and not making the right decision. Why was I getting threatening letters and now a dead cat on my doorstep? And the biggest question of them all: Where was Peyton with my child? My mind was going a mile a minute and it seemed like all the solution lead back to one place, home.

With my eyes closed I tried to think of anything else except what I had to deal with when I got back. Reaching around in my purse I felt the edges of an envelope that I had been given before I left NY. Turning it over in my hands, it was a handwritten note from Ali. The script was neat and business like him. It made me smile to think he took the time out to actually write something on paper, because the art of hand writing was almost dead because of technology. Even though he told me to wait until I got home to open it, my curiosity got the best of me. Slipping my finger between the papers, I ripped open the top. Looking inside I was surprised to see that not only was it letter but it was check inside also. My eyes had to be deceiving me because it was way too many zeros for him to just give to me as a tip. God worked in mysterious ways; I would never look the gift horse in the mouth. I was grateful for life that I lived even if it wasn't what it always should be.

Hands shaking, I tried to unfold the letter without tearing the words. As I read the words that were written, I knew that trouble never lasted always. That even though it seems like the end, it could just be the beginning of something special.

Dear Kennedy,

I know that we just met, and that it wasn't under the best or ideal circumstances. In that brief period of time I felt like I've known you forever. Sometimes you meet someone and you just click, well that's how I felt when I met you. Maybe it was the drugs and the booze or maybe it was just your personality shining through, but I see a good person who is going through a bad time. I know this may come as surprise, me cutting you that check. I have my reasons why, and that small amount will make your life so much easier. I spoke with my close friend and confidant who I told you to contact if you needed help, he told me a little about you and your situation. It seems as if life just wants to keep knocking you down, but time after time you have picked yourself back up and kept it moving. I hope that the money can help you get to where you need to be. I have enclosed the business card of the man that can help you if need be. I hope that everything works out in your favor.

Best Wishes

Ali

P.S I know that La Jefa has a strict policy on receive tips and gifts. This is neither nor, this is between us.

Looking into the envelope, I also found an all black business card. The front was embossed in gold with only three lines on it.

Myles R Lear
Security Specialist
(634) 764-2130

I wasn't exactly sure what I needed his services for but I would keep the card just in case. Tears started to well up in my eyes; you never knew where your next blessing was coming from. When I took this job, it was just a means to the end. Now I see how being in this position allowed me to meet people who would never speak to me, let alone help me. I stuck the card in the inside pocket of my wallet along with the check. I was ready to rest my eyes, but decided to send Ali a thank you text. And as the wheels went up and all electronic devices were ordered to be turned off, I seen that the text was sent. With my head back, I knew this was probably the last time that I would sleep this fitful for a while.

CHAPTER 10
All Good Things...........

Being awoken to the sound of the attendant telling me to sit upright and put on your seat belt is disorientated. First I couldn't remember where I was and what was going on. Then the reality of the disarray of my life started to play across my brain. My eyes closed in NYC and opened up at ACY. My body felt tired but my mind felt alert. The feeling of impending doom was so strong that if I didn't get high I would jump out of my skin. Standing on the tarmac, I looked like I had money but was more broke than the workers milling around me. Grabbing my luggage, I was in a rush to get home. Overnight bag, purse and rolling luggage had me bogged down. It was time to hit the ground running and make shit happen. Reaching in my purse I pulled out my phone. As soon as I turned it on it was like the world started to orbit again. All types of alerts started coming through, text messages, emails, and voicemail all vying for my attention. My phone was only off for almost 2 hours, you would've thought that I had been out of commission for days instead of hours. Walking with my head down, scrolling through the text messages, I wanted to see if anything changed in the last hour or so. Engrossed in trying to get through my messages I a heard a voice calling out to me, "Hey Kennedy!"

I turned to walk right into the broad chest of a tall, handsome well dressed man. His smile was alluring and stunning. His eyes gave me the impression that we met before but I couldn't remember exactly where. By his tone, it seemed as if he already knew me.

"Hi I'm Miles, Ali sent me. He said I might be of service to you. I'm a security specialist. Can I help you with your bags?" He said taking my luggage and handing me my purse back.

"How did you know who I was and where to find me? He told me that your contact information was just in case I needed it." I said mesmerized by the way he was looking at me.

"To be honest, after he gave me your info and looked into your situation, I seen some things that told me that you would definitely be needing me. Is there somewhere we can go that is private and talk about it?" he gestured around the airport with hordes of people walking around us.

"Sure, we can go to my place. I need to check my house first." I said. He escorted me to the curb and had a rental vehicle waiting for us. My mind raced a mile a minute thinking of the implications of the small conversation we just had. What did he mean when he said some things that I would need help sorting out? He slid behind the driver seat and took the wheel like a pro. His presence was so big that it felt like he took up the whole car with his charming allure. I wasn't getting any bad vibes from him like he wanted to harm me. In fact I couldn't pick up any vibes from him, he was overall a professional. Looking over at him he seemed at ease, like he didn't have a care in the world. You tell that just under the surface was a strong masculinity waiting to surface. It made me think that he was either good at hiding his emotions or a master of disguise.

"I was surprised to hear someone calling me in the airport since no one was expecting me. I was supposed to be away until the end of the week, I had to cut my trip way short. And then to find out Ali sent you, I was really surprised. He told me to contact you if I needed help, he must know something that I don't know." I said watching the cars fly past my car window.

"Can I be honest? Ali gave me your name and I did a little research. It's not hard when you have a high security clearance. It makes it easy to find out about people, they're lifestyles, and the things that they prefer. After I emailed him the small report I made, he said that you needed more than you thought. He was adamant about me being here to meet you at the airport." Myles said without taking his eyes off the road.

We drove in silence while I let his words soak in. Ali had someone run a security check on me? That was invasive as hell, but I guess when you have a lot to lose you don't risk it over someone you barely know. And what was on that report that made him feel compelled to send a specialist to meet me? The closer I got to home the more I felt my anxiety flaring up. I was zoning, trying to make sense of the pieces of the puzzle that I could see. But before my thoughts could get to deep, my phone rang alerting me to an incoming call.

Looking at the caller ID, the number flashing across the screen was unrecognizable. On edge with everything, I was never into answering numbers I didn't know. Thinking better against it I answered.

"Hello Kennedy. I'm sorry to hear that you had to leave NY unexpectedly due to some family problems. Your sister made me aware of what was going on and what you needed to handle immediately. You know that I have a strict policy of not paying when you don't complete a job assignment. I hate to disappoint clients or lose money behind a chick that can't handle her business well enough that she needs to leave work early. That is one of the reasons we usually don't hire people with children. They make it difficult for you to focus on the task on hand versus worrying about your child's welfare. But that is neither here nor there. There are also other consequences that also occur besides not getting paid, but since I spoke with Ali I have changed my course of action. You must have done something good to him for him to put in a good word for you. And since he is one of my top clients, I will honor his wishes in order to keep his business." La Jefa stated matter of factly.

I didn't know what to say. I didn't know how much Myles knew or could hear but I could feel his eyes peering a hole into the side of my head. She made me speechless, I was afraid to find out what the other consequences were since I didn't follow the rules, but I was happy that I wouldn't find out either. It seemed as if Ali's reach extended farther than his business, I was grateful to have made his acquaintance.

"Thank you! I know that I could have conducted myself better, but some situations are completely out of my hands. To be honest I still don't know what exactly is going on. I hope to have a solution ASAP and be able to come back to NY. I appreciate you bending the rules for me, I promise not to let you down. That money is really important to my well being and I would like a chance to earn my keep." I said at a loss for words. I didn't know which way this conversation was going; I hoped that it went in my favor.

"There is no need to apologize; your funds have already been deposited since he paid the full amount even though you didn't stay. You lucked up this time. Handle your business, and contact me when you're available. Make it sooner than later, because I have a line of girls waiting to have an opportunity to make a lot of money. Later." She said before hanging up the phone in my ear.

"Is everything ok?" Blake asked as he pulled up in my driveway.

As he came to a halt, it just occurred to me that I never told him where I lived or gave him directions, he just knew. Turning to ask how he knew, he put his hand up to stop me from speaking." When I said I looked into your life, I did. That included your address and phone number. Don't be alarmed, let's go in and have a talk. I'll grab your bags, just open the door."

My mind wouldn't allow me to think past the next 5 minutes, let alone to any future events. My only focus right now was to find my child. I just mumbled an ok and grabbed my purse looking for my keys. As I approached the door, the alarm bells ringing in my head got louder. Like a mini warning beacon that was making the hair on my arms stand on edge, the goose bumps making me shiver like I was standing out in the cold versus in the summer sun. Touching the knob to get a grip, the door squeaked open without me using my key. I knew something was amiss, because I knew that I double checked everything before I left knowing I would be gone a while.

"Step back; let me take a look first." Myles said shielding me from entering a possibly dangerous situation. I let him take the lead while walking in behind him the first thing that hit was the fragrance. The sickly sweet smell of being in a florist shop invaded my senses. Thousands upon thousands of dead roses covered the floor. Every surface that I looked at was covered in the dead petals. Even though I was told to stay close behind Myles my curiosity got the best of me and my feet moved on their own accord. The need to know everything was over powering my brain to focus on anything else. I had to see what else was going on in my house. My phone rang, it was my sister. I rejected the call and texted her I would call her back, I was handling some business. Nothing was out of place expected for the thousands of roses littering my house. I couldn't understand what the flowers meant but it was creepy. Now I was concerned because how did they get into the house without breaking in? The thought flitted across my mind that my mom had come over to check the mail and found the dead cat on my porch. She could have easily been distracted when she opened the package, and forgot to lock up correctly. Yet and still who had enough gumption to come in my space without permission? Reaching for my phone I needed to make sure that she locked the door.

"Wait, I think there is something that you need to see." He said leading me back into the living room. On top of the mantle was a card with my name written on the front, the writing seemed familiar but at the same time I really didn't know what to expect.

Opening the letter, my hands shook and trembled. I was scared, I was nervous; I was coming down after being on a steady Coke, alcohol, and Xanax diet. I was withdrawing and trying to focus on the task at hand at the same damn time. It was hard, but as I lifted the flap I knew that what I would read could possibly kill me.

Sometimes people are fortunate enough to get
the things in life that others dream of.
These people tend to take the gift bestowed amongst
them as fleeting fancy that can be easily replaced.
These people also take and hurt from the
people who love them the most.
It's all fun and games until those things are gone.
You can't bear a seed of doubt and deception and expect to get fruit.
All you get Kennedy is what you give.
You give dirt and then cry a river to end up swimming in mud.
Revenge is to even the score.

The rage just bubbled up inside of me. The last line of the letter rolled around in my head, "Revenge is to even the score." What score and who would want revenge on me? I never did anything intentional to hurt or harm anyone. I trembled as I reread the letter again, not totally making sense of the situation or what the writer was trying to say. Did someone hurt my best friend and daughter to get back at me? The thought made my stomach turn so fast that I could taste the bile rising up in my throat. Running to the sink, I dry heaved my empty stomach.

"We have to go to my best friend's house and see if I can find anything out. This is crazy; I don't know who would want revenge on me." I said as the tears started to trickle down my face. Deciding to check the rest of the house before I left to see if anything jumped out at me, I headed for the steps. Walking from room to room, everything looked fine. Peeking in baby girl's room, it looked scarce, but then I remembered she came and got some of her things to take to Peyton's house. Picking up one of her dolls off the floor, I fixed her clothes and sat her back on the dresser next to her picture collection. When I decorated her room, I felt it would be best if she had pictures that reflected happy family memories so that she would always be surrounded with love. Touching each frame, all of the pictures were still here except the pictures of her and her father. It was odd, because I never recalled her taking those with her. Maybe in one of my states of not knowing, she asked and I agreed.

Going into my bedroom, I found my secret stash. Grabbing the contents, I was between a rock and a hard place. I said I was going to kick my habit because it was ruining my whole life. But I was so stressed out at the moment I knew that one hit would ease some of the angst that I was feeling. Just as I was going to lay out a line, I could feel his footsteps on the hallway carpet.

"Is everything ok? Are you ready to go?' Myles asked looking at me with suspicious eyes.

Stuffing the drugs into my pocket, I turned and looked him in his eyes, "Yes, let's go. I got distracted is all?" Pulling my bedroom door shut, we checked all the windows and doors before we locked up to make sure everything was secure for certain this time.

Getting back into the passenger side, pulling my shades down, I could see my next door neighbor talking to the old lady that lived across the street. I could tell they were talking about me by the way that they just kept sneaking glances at me. Or maybe it wasn't me, maybe it was him. His aura was so bright that your eyes just gravitated towards him. Myles was in deep conversation on his cell pacing up and down my driveway. Whatever he was talking about in hushed tones must have been serious based on the look on his face. I was trying to make out what he was saying but he kept turning his back so I couldn't read his lips. I took in his swag while he wasn't watching and impressive. He was a good looking man to say the least, the type of dude that made you argue with your friends about staying with even if he was a piece of shit. He wore his clothes fitted and neat, not loose and baggy like a dope boy, and you could see the confidence oozing out of his pores like he owned this whole block. I was attracted to him, but my attraction felt wrong with everything going on. I had a hunger for men and it seemed like it didn't matter the circumstances or time, the attraction would still find a place to take root. I tried to shake the thoughts but I couldn't help it. I knew that if he decided to pursue me in any capacity I would be with it. Hearing the car door slam brought me back to reality somewhat, but the feeling in the pit of my stomach was fluttering.

"Is everything ok?" I asked as he pulled out of the driveway and headed toward Peyton's house.

"Actually, something is wrong. I just got a call from one of my sources that told me something disturbing. I would rather wait and discuss it after we check your friend's house." He said not making eye contact with me. I knew then that something was seriously wrong that he wasn't telling me. I tried to call Peyton again to no avail, I rang her job and they said she went on a sabbatical. They had no idea when she was coming back and didn't really care because she could do her job from wherever she was. She didn't need to show up every day as long as she emailed all off her assignments in.

I tried to be calm as we pulled up, but I could tell from the outside that the house was lifeless. It had a cold distant feeling like no happiness or laughter had ever been in this place. Taking out my key I opened the lock and stepped inside with Myles quick on my heels.

All of the furniture was covered in sheets, there were no personal affects lying around. It looked as if someone had packed up all the important stuff and left the furniture only. I raced from room to room while Myles was telling me to calm down. But as I reached another room and another, each one feeling less homey than the last, my face became crestfallen. I knew as soon as I opened Samina's room door that they were gone.

All of Samina stuff was gone, all of her clothes, pictures she had drawn, and toys were gone. The only thing in the room was the canopy bed that Peyton had purchased just for her. Sitting in the middle of the floor in my daughter's room the tears started to fall. That's when I looked up and seen Myles face, and his look said he already knew what happened before we even arrived. He wanted to give me the opportunity to see it with my own two eyes.

"My source says that Peyton boarded a plan to Minami with your daughter 2 hours after you left. I also found out that she had withdrawn all of the money that she had in the bank. It seems like she had been planning this for a while. They lost track of her once she got on plane. I found this letter for you on the kitchen counter. I'll be downstairs." He said as he handed me the letter. Our hands touched and in that brief moment a jolt of electricity shot up my arm and our eyes met. I could see in his eyes that he felt what I felt, attraction. I turned away hoping that he wouldn't see the lust in my eyes but I could feel my checks heating thru his stare.

Opening the letter, I prepared for the worse, but the worse couldn't prepare me for what I was about to read.

Kennedy

We have been friends more like sisters since we were kids. I have loved you like my own and treated you like the sister I never had. We always seemed to have each other's back thru ups and downs. We even slit our thumbs and pressed them together so that we could be blood sisters and always have a bond. Everything was cool until you did the one thing that I never expected. You stole my dude. And no I'm not talking about Blake, I'm talking about Carlos. The summer that you went to stay with your aunt was when we first met. I was so sad to be stuck in the city while you went on a country adventure; all I did was sulk around. That was until Los and his family moved in around the corner from me. He was so young and cute; I knew that I wanted to be with him. So that summer we hang every day, he gave me something to look forward to until you came back. The more we hung out the more I liked him and I thought he felt the same way. I could tell he liked me too, but we were young and didn't know what to do with our hormones raging out of control. So the day before you came back, I ended up losing my virginity to him under the steps of my porch in my backyard. I was so excited to have finally lost my virginity I couldn't wait for you to see me to see if you noticed something different. That night I barely slept thinking of the look on your face when you seen me. But I was so wound up that when I finally fell asleep, I ended up oversleeping. When I woke up, I got dressed and was rushed out the door to get to your house. Only to find you sitting on my porch talking to Carlos like y'all had already knew each other. Laughing and giggling like y'all were fast friends. Y'all were so busy staring at each other that it took for me to clear my throat for you to even notice me. But I could already see that he liked you more than he ever liked me. Instead of me speaking up, I let him choose, and he chose you. It crushed me, but I never stopped loving him. He was the one that got away, and you didn't deserve him. I thought you would just be a thing and he would see that I am the better woman but he didn't. So I just played the background acting like I was happy for you when really I was envious. Then I found out when I was 19 that I would never be able to have kids, and while I was dealing with that, you ended up pregnant. See you told me everything, but never listened or paid attention to what I had going on. I didn't feel the need to share the info with you because; hey it wouldn't have made a difference. It took me years to realize just how self centered and selfish you really are. So when Los came to me crying about how all you do is party and leave the baby with him, the house is always a wreck, and all you were worried about was you, I used that to my advantage. I wanted to be with him so bad that I would take him any way that I could have him. Even if that meant that I could have him sometimes. See because even though he was with you, I knew he really wasn't happy. I knew that I was everything that you were not. But you had a baby and that was something I couldn't do. So when he got locked up and I seen how loose you were, I knew it was time to make a move. I started visiting him the weeks you didn't go, I made sure his commissary was always full, and most of all I loved his daughter better than you could. See the plan was to leave you and bring Samina while we ride off into the sunset and leave you to do whatever you wanted to. But the plan back fired when he felt like he wanted to teach you a lesson. He ended up dead, and I was heartbroken all over again. It felt like he had been taken away from me all over again, but this time I knew that there was no chance of things being different or us starting a life together away from everyone. I mastered the Spanish language and even taught Mina too. I had been saving money at every turn under the guise that my real life was about to start. But just like everything you touch, it always fails or breaks or dies. It was no way that I would let anything happen to Mina because she was my last link to him. After he died and I grieved my heart out I knew that I had to follow thru for baby girl's sake. She needed me more than ever since her mother was boozing and getting high most of the time and couldn't focus on anything except herself. You made it easy for me, you gave me custody, you let Mina move in with me, and you made me more important to her than you were. And then you slept with Blake, instead of you leaving him alone you still crept with him behind my back after I confronted you. What type of friend, let alone best friend would do that to their own friend? Kennedy, because Kennedy only thinks about herself. So now you have all the time and means to do you. Like I said, revenge is a dish best served cold.

Peyton
P.S If you weren't so wrapped up in your own shit
you would have been noticed that I didn't really
fuck with you like that you Coke Whore

A gut wrench sob escaped out of my mouth as I crumbled to the floor in angst. I was in the middle of the biggest breakdown in my life when the epiphany final registered. That whore, Karma, had come back around. She bitch slapped me across the face and made me take heed to her constant warnings. The thoughts on how my selfish acts had lead me to this point. The realization of that made me cry all that much harder. And then that's when I knew that all the letters, and dead cats, and roses were all her. Peyton had been systematically breaking me down for the last 10 months to get her way. But I was so dense and wrapped up in my own world that it never beeped on my radar. Now I would pay the ultimate price by losing my daughter.

I sat in the same spot without moving until the sun went down and the shadows played across the walls. Myles was somewhere else in the house because I could feel his presence and hear whispers of the constant conversation he was having on his cell. I was so zoned out that I didn't realize he was in front of me until I looked up.

"Are you ok?" he whispered.

"No."

"Well pack a bag. We're going to Miami to get your daughter back." Myles.

ACKNOWLEDGEMENTS

First, I want to thank God for blessing me with the ability of storytelling and the mind to string two words together that actually make since. I know without Him, there is no me. I appreciate all the gifts bestowed upon me, and I pray that he keeps working on me so that I can reach my full potential.

I want to thank my sons, Julian Echevarria-Hunter and Jaydin Echevarria for being the reason I am constantly trying to better myself. I know y'all watched me have a lot of late nights and earlier mornings chasing my dream. Not only have you all been my inspiration but you've also loved me unconditional because I have loved you unconditionally. Thank you for understanding that mom is always chasing the money for you all, and thank you for loving on me when I didn't love myself. You are both the best parts of me and I wouldn't trade you guys for all the Turkey Hill Iced Tea in the world! I LOVE YOU GUYS MORE THAN LIFE ITSELF, YOU MAKE THIS LIFE WORTH LIVING!

To my stepchildren, Jamaira Echevarria-Soto and Julio Echevarria-Soto, I love you like I birthed you. I am happy that I got a chance to watch you grow up into the young adults that you are today. I am so proud of all of your accomplishments and I can't wait to see what life brings you. Keep being Great.

To Jose Echevarria aka Cook. Thank you for supporting me even when you had no clue what I was trying to do. I know I can be a pain, stubborn, moody, bull headed, strong minded, strong willed, and overall just a jerk! But you always listened to me (even if it was a dumb ass conversation about shit you didn't care about). I hope life moves out of your way and you get everything you deserve. Thank you for always trying to love me.

To my sister Jameelah bka Mimi (no one ever calls her by her real name unless they just met her!) We have been inseparable since birth, connected at the hip and heart. Thank you for listening to my dumb ass rants about inconsequential bullshit that has no meaning. And for always being on my side supporting all of y crazy ideas and ambitions. I love you twin face!

To the rest of my sisters: Atiya, Quantay, Malikah, and Naeemah. Life would be sooooo dull without you guys. It's never a dull moment and it's always exciting, especially when you're the middle sister. Love Y'all Janky asses, I wouldn't want any other sisters!

For my brothers: Kareem, Dane, Tony, Darryl, Rennie, Demetrius, Isaiah, Jamil, Ibn Ishmial Khalid, Armani, Amir, and Amore: We not see eye to eye or even agree all the time. Near or far, I love you all too. Thank You for always being there for me, for being straight Goons and never ever letting anyone do anything to me.

To my mom, Trina thank you for bussing it open for a real dude my dad, George. Without y'all I wouldn't be here.

Special Thank You to my cousins: Jamillah, Jahi, and Jareef Hunter: No need for a long soliloquy, just know that even when I thought I couldn't finish, y'all always pushed and encouraged me. Always uplifting and pushing me up, up, up. From humble beginnings, we're going all the way to the top.

To my handful of friends(More Like sister's) Doneesha Cross (Hey Bestie since Before Breasts), Lorraine Meijas, Katrina Chaney, Shameka

Ravenell, and Christina Golden. We may not speak everyday or see each other as much as we would like but I appreciate every one of your friendships. All unique, strong goal orientated women, y'all keep me inspired. And answer the phone whenever I'm up burning the midnight oil or just beat. We have had some times, collectively and separately that can never be mentioned! We share secrets that will go to the grave and never uttered! I can't wait to see how much more our relationships develop with time.

To Kyle Sears, who straight told me to my face just do it, not to be a punk bitch! Even when I thought this book was going to be shit, you said it was going to be sugar. And you only gave me 5 minutes a day to be emotional, than told me to suck that shit up! Thanks for the push!

To my nieces and nephews: Ahnajah, Anirah, Roen, Riley, Amatullah, Kareema, Eniyah, Madison, Quannie, Lil Kareem, Perry, Rashaun, Bilal, Lil Dane, and Cobei. The future is bright with y'all in it. Be inspired, be encouraged, go far and be great. I love you all!!!!

Special Shot Out to my Girlie Deanna Downs, I would have loved to share this opportunity with you. We shared a love for books that was uncomparable to any other bond. Your gone but never ever forgotten.

To my Golden Nugget Family(The job that pays me to fund my dream) Angel, Bob, Bharat, Ishvar, Ari, James, Dan B, Raj, Carlos, Julietta, Jake, Jose, Moises, Shalim, Sheri, Mery, Stephanie, Wendy, Dixie, Ms. Eloise, Mrs. Pam, Wellington, Benny, Big Juan, Lil Juan, Bill, Frank, and all the Chef's. Y'all have cooked for me, laughed with me, gave me suggestion, listened to me, encouraged and inspired me. Even as I type this y'all are calling me! I might hate the politics of the company but I love my peoples. To my boss, Dan Kelleher, who has worked with and around my schedule, let me vent until I was over it, stuffed me with snacks, left me alone to do my homework to get my degree and watched me toil over this novel. I appreciate you my dude, even though you're an op cause your upper management. You never got on a power trip and always let me be without asking me to change. I know my mouth is horrible at times, but you never shut my shit down. Thanks Guys!!!!!

To my hairstylist Treva Barnes @ElementsOfHair You have been blessing my scalp for over 15 years. Thanks for always, I mean always accommodating me. With those early early appojntments and super late just to hook my doo up! When I make it big, I swear I'm taking you with me on the road.

To anyone that I forgot, it was never intentional, I swear. I appreciate each and every one of you. Next book you in there like swimwear.

ABOUT THE AUTHOR

Khalidah J Hunter was born and raised in Atlantic City, New Jersey. When she's not daydreaming about fairies and world peace, she's curled up with her favorite book, headphones bumping Pandora, and trying to be normal. If she's not at her day job, she's enjoying her real job of raising her two handsome sons. She currently resides in South Jersey where you wear flip flops until October and hit the beach at the end of May.

Printed in the United States
By Bookmasters